Reviews

Valley of the Yellow Stones is a book of artistry and will become a best seller without doubt.

Phillip Davis, PhD

A well written book blended with humor and tragic war tales.

Dr. G. Mason

Charlotte and Pattimari have a great imagination and it shows in their stories.

Jeanne Trachman

What I really enjoy about your story among other qualities is that the characters are everymen. They are not specific cultures so as to make your story's universal and fundamental human truths relevant to a diverse audience. It says much about you as an author appealing to a higher conscious and wisdom; very cosmopolite in its approach. Though a morality and cautionary tale, there is a fable like sense of wonder as well.

Greg Patrick, Facebook

Pmsd/ChJ

The Valley of the Yellow Stones

First book in series of three

Published by Lulu Publishing

ISBN 978-0-359-57287-8

First Edition

Contents

Authors

Pattimari Sheets-Cacciolfi resides in California; her field is psychology, her thrill is writing, and gardening is where you'll find her most sunny days - where she creates the characters of her books and is inspiration from her nature friends.

Charlotte Huston-Johnson resides in California. Her creativity soars to the highest level and she enjoys developing scenes where her characters come alive with magical descriptions.

Co-Authors

Donnie Anderson and Melissa Dudley-Anderson reside in California where they let their imagination soar to its highest level. They came aboard as our co-writers because they had such creative ideas and scene descriptions that Char, and I added them as co-authors.

Foreword ☼

Ancient History of Valley of the Yellow Stones

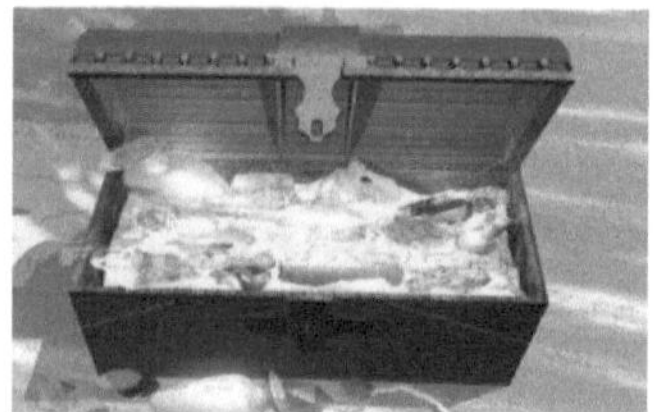

There was a valley in the land of the ancients called Sheran and later renamed the Valley of the Yellow Stones. Its name came from the large yellow stones that were discovered in the streams, lakes, and rivers. Back in ancient times, the yellow stones were so plentiful that the ancients made jewelry and gold coins with them to barter with the surrounding villages and towns. They accumulated such a vast amount of riches that their greed overpowered their love for the land and stripped it of its minerals and nutrients; altering the rivers, lakes, and soil; leaving the land barren. Even with all their vast riches, the villagers were slowly and painfully starving to death so the Shaman Gershwen, came up with a plan to give back to the land and end their greediness. He called a village meeting, and soon after arriving they seated themselves on the ground in front of Gershwen; he began speaking. "Our people are starving, and we need to give back to the earth for in our greediness we've taken far too much; leaving our land unproductive."

One of the stone-smiths yelled out, "How do we give back what is no longer?"

"Good question Smitz, I'm about to tell you. I plan to have each one of you stone-smiths design the finest golden egg ever imaged. In order to create such an egg, it must come from your heart and soul. Each egg must be carved into a beautiful detailed piece of art."

"Gershwen, we're jewelry-makers, not artist," Bellowed out the finest jewelry-maker of the village.

"Hold on, Jerwin, I'll explain, and don't think for a moment you aren't an artist; what you do is art of the finest."

"Okay, Shaman Gershwen, if you say so," Responded Jerwin.

"I not only say so, but I also speak the truth. Okay, now what I want each one of you thirteen jewelry-makers to do is like I mentioned before; put your heart and soul into the design, and you have one week to complete this task."

Jerwin scratched his head and said, "Gershwen, one week?"

"If need be, two weeks, but not a day longer, "Gershwen responded.

The men scurried off to begin their requested task by collecting the finest yellow stones they could find. They worked eight days and nights producing their finest details imagined in their minds with their whole heart and soul, and a flawless egg was created. Satisfied with their creation, they polished them into a luminous shine, and then stood back and beamed at their miraculous work.

As the villagers gathered, weak from hunger, Gershwen said, "On the next full moon, the thirteen jewelry-makers will bury the awe-inspiring eggs as an offering to the land, and I will cast my magic on the eggs, and the land in this valley will be healed. It will then produce the finest crops around, and water will be plentiful; trees will come alive and bare the sweetest fruit in the land. Fish will again swim in the land's waters and send out their miraculous liveliness to all of our people."

The next full moon the village people gathered in the valley, and each one of the thirteen jewelry-makers buried their egg.

After they were finished, Shaman Gershwen stood in the center of the valley, drew a circle on the ground, placed stones in the center while sage and frankincense were burning, then clasped his hands together and said, "With smoke and flame of the stars, moon, and sun, let the healing power begin. Let the earth be whole; heal the outside and heal within. Land, sea, fire, and wind make mankind begin to care. Heal the wounds of the great mother-earth and let the power of healing begin." Gershwen began chanting, and a bright glowing light blasted out from his hands and when he unclasped them the light expanded all over the valley. When it ended, and the valley was tranquil again; the winds stopped. The people cried out. "Land we have given our creation from thirteen artist's hands; forgive us for being greedy. Forgive us land!"

The next morning when the sun launched its light over the village, all villagers went to the lake and shouted in gladness at what they saw; water in the lake and fish were jumping out of the water sending their astonishing energy to all the village people. Dancing villagers began to thank the land with tears flooding down their faces. In the darkness of the night, a roaring campfire, big as a small village hut, sent out its warmth and the festival began. Smoked fish in their stomachs and regained strength; they rejoiced in their dance and cried in gladness. Many jumped in the river and lifted their hands to the heavens and shouted, "We shall always give back to you, earth, and we will never take our land and riches for granted again."

Gershwen shouted out to the people that the buried eggs would never be mentioned again, and it was to remain a secret for as long as they lived. "When the time comes, thousands of years from now, villagers will find the eggs, and it will be our bequest to them. They will see the writings in the caves and know these eggs are sacred; giving perfect weather conditions."

As time went by, the crops flourish, and the villagers were happy. So happy that they built two thirteen feet statues to stand on each side of their village's entrance, holding a golden egg and spear in each hand to remind them of the hardship they endured for being greedy and not thinking of the land's needs.

Valley of the Yellow Stones ll

Chapter One ☼

The Stolen Sacred Golden Eggs

There was a valley in the land of the ancients called Sheran, and later renamed the Valley of the Yellow Stones. Its name came from ancient peoples who left a legacy to many generations to come. On the cave walls it described the large yellow stones that were discovered in the streams, lakes, and rivers and the secret the Sheran people kept till death; the greed they had and how it affected their land.

With the new generations as was in the ancient times, the yellow stones were so plentiful that the valley's men made jewelry and gold coins with them. They'd put the stones into wooden carts and oxen would pull the heavy load around the mountain where they'd separate the stones and melt them into golden bars.

It was a cold day in the early part of winter with sprinkles of snow covering the hills with clouds hanging dark and gloomy over the village miners as they pulled their wooden carts in the early morning's dawning, and each early morning, the first thing they saw was the pale gleam of yellow stones.

The village women were busy cooking for the miners knowing the magistrate would deliver their food in a wagon. But that cold, gloomy day, Cetus, was sick with a fever and his sons were busy chopping wood, so he asked his young daughter, Jasmine, to take his place and make the delivery. She had traveled with her father on several occasions, so she knew the journey well. Even though Cetus was worried about his daughter going alone, he had no other alternative but to let her go.

"Father, don't worry, I'm twenty years old now, and don't forget I've gone with you many times, so I will make the journey just fine."

"I know Jasmine, but a father can still worry about his daughter, can't he?"

Jasmine grinned sweetly and placed an affectionate kiss on her father's whiskered cheek then quickly began loading the wagon to take the long two-hour journey. She always took her ferrets with her wherever she went because they were her friends and great companions. All three ferrets tucked snuggly in her leather shoulder pouch were ready for the long trip. Each had a name, and when she addressed them, they immediately responded. Jazzel was her favorite because she was the lady of the three. Cosmos was always playing tricks on everyone which made Jasmine laugh at his funny behavior. Philo was the serious one and would snuggle up to Jasmine when she needed quiet moments.

As the oxen headed down the road, pulling the wagon, her father bellowed out, "Jasmine, be careful, it's going to be a mighty cold day."

She looked back and gave her father a broad smile as she yelled back, "Okay, father, I will."

Cetus knew his daughter was older than her young years because her grandmother who was the shaman of the village had taught her well. One day she would stand in her grandmother's place, and he knew she was a wise daughter and would get the food delivered in a timely manner.

Jasmine was an attractive woman with long dark wavy hair and a creamy olive complexion that complimented her ocean blue eyes. Her eyes showed wisdom, and many felt she knew everything about them when she looked into their eyes. She was loved by the village people because she was always happy with a song in her heart. All the men had great respect for her because they knew she had been taught to defend herself and could handle a sword as good as any man. When she rode on a horse she flew like the wind with class and style, but strength. All the village people knew she was no one to be reckoned with, but they also knew she knew how to be feminine too.

Her father often said she was delicate and sweet as an angel, but strong and wise as a tiger. She never missed giving her parents a big hug and kiss when she went away on journeys.

Jasmine looked back and saw her father waving. She blew him a kiss and then turned back around, giggling. She was excited and happy about helping her father.

When Jasmine arrived, the miners were shouting with happiness and were very pleased to see her.

"Hi Jasmine, where's your father?"

"He's down with the fever, but he'll be fine soon. I took his place so you hard working men could eat." She laughed quietly and helped the men unload the wagon.

They all cheered as they gather round to eat and filled up their hungry bellies.

After the meal was gulped down, Jasmine loaded up her things and was getting ready to leave when the miners told her to stay a while longer; at least until it was safe to go home. As it turned out the snow didn't stop so, she spent the night instead of trying to get through the snowy slush.

When Jasmine woke up early the next morning, she moved Philo aside then stood up and prepared for departure. She was eager to get home and trusted her parents understood her overnight stay.

After traveling what seemed like hours, she could see the village off into the distance, but she didn't see the two tall statues that always stood leading into the village's entrance. A light kindled in the heavens, an inferno of orange fire. She screamed in fear as she shrunk back, afraid for a moment. "Oh no! The village has been attacked!" As she moved closer, she noticed a blazing fire. "Fire! Oh, I must hurry." She screamed for her oxen to go faster and as she approached the village, she cried out, "Oh, no!" She could see the destruction clearly as she jumped off the wagon and hollered out with her hands high in the air running around in circles and crying. "Where are you father? Mother! Grandmother! Where are you?" The village had been burned almost to the ground, and all that was left was burning ashes and the last few buildings blazing.

She rubbed her eyes with the back of her hand and then ran to her father's house. She immediately saw his body lying in the slushy mud with his hand frozen in her mother's as she lay dead with an arrow in her back. She threw herself over her parents' bodies and weep. "Oh, father, oh, father, I'm so sorry I wasn't here to help you. Oh, mother, I'm so sorry."

She jumped up and ran to the neighboring hut and saw Jacob, the eldest in the village, dying on the ground as he struggled to tell Jasmine about the attack.

"Jasmine…it…it…was the Vikons who…who attacked us. They torched and burned down the village and tore down our sacred temple. They…they took our alabaster cup with our sacred golden eggs made from the finest gold. Our statues have been knocked to the ground. They…" His head fell back, and his eyes closed.

"Oh…oh…this is terrible. Those eggs are thousands of years old, buried here by the ancients; a bequest to us." She looked down and noticed the old man had died. She pushed herself up and looked around at all the obliteration, in sorrow.

The thirteen eggs had been in two small wooden boxes made of the finest teak wood with sacred carvings on the handles. It was gone, along with the sacred eggs which represented equinox; the summer and winter solstice, handed down by the ancients. The carvings on them were with great detail and brilliance done by the ancients and given magical power by the Great Ancient Shaman Gershwen to protect the land in the Valley of the Yellow Stones. Each egg told the story of how they balanced the earth and had special powers and was pathways to knowledge. Only a few of the village people knew how to use the special powers to heal and change the weather so crops could grow. Fortunately, Jasmine knew, so if she could find the eggs, the village would breathe life again. Yes, they'd have to rebuild it and they would.

It was important for the eggs to not end up in the wrong hands because it could bring down all villages around.

She looked around for her grandmother but didn't see her anywhere, so she ran from place to place looking and shouting, "Grandmother! Grandmother!"

Jasmine saw movement in the cornfield and stood frozen. She didn't know if she imagined the figure, she saw a swirl and turn or if it was the smoke that turned black and stormed up in circles to the heavens. It was misty with blackness. Wilted with fear that it could be the Vikons, she crawled to the cellar which she knew was in the field. It was where she played as a child and that's where she saw her grandmother lying on the ground, still alive, but unconscious. "Grandmother, wake up, wake up. Oh, Grandmother, you've got to live. I can't handle all of this obliteration without you!" Jasmine sat down beside her grandmother; willing her to wake up. She remembered all the stories her grandmother had told her and now she lay unconscious. Jasmine sat in despair at all the damage and now her grandmother lying unconscious threw her off balance without directness as to what she should do. Although Jasmine had been told all of her grandmother's stories over and over again, she loved to hear the one she always begged her grandmother to tell again and again; about the old woman who lived in a hidden place that everyone knew, but few had ever seen. As the story always went; in those great days the old woman seemed to wait for lost or wandering people and seekers to come to her place. She was circumspect, hairy, always fat, and especially wished to avoid most people's company unless she was needed. She was both a crower and a cackler, generally having more animal sounds than human ones. Her grandmother had told her that she lived among the rotten granite slopes in Taramumara Indian territory and was buried outside of it near a well. It was said that she traveled continuously looking for lost souls. Her cave was filled with bones of all manner of desert creatures; the deer, rattlesnake, and the crow, but her specialty was wolves. She crept and crawled through the mountains and dry riverbeds, looking for wolf bones and then assembled them into a skeleton. When she had the last bone in place and the beautiful white sculpture was finished, she'd sit by the fire and sing. Some people said some of her skeletons would come alive and help her search for the wounded souls that needed her magical powers. It was said that if you wandered the desert, and it was near sundown, and a little bit lost, and mighty tired, then you are lucky, for she would show you things; something of a soul, especially if she took a liking to you. Jasmine's grandmother told her that she was called many names, but the one that she liked best was LaBoba, the wild woman, who lived in the desert. Some called her Mother-Creator who controlled the skies and winds and the thoughts of humans from which all reality spread. LaBoba knew the ancient past for she survived generation after generation and was old beyond time. She was the archivist of feminine intention and her whiskers sense the future; she had a far-seeing milky eye of the old crone; she lived backward and forward in time simultaneously, correcting for one side by dancing with the other. It is believed that she lives within those in need and thrives in the deepest soul-psyche of women, the ancient and vital Wild Woman. It is said her home was that place in time where the spirit of women and the spirit of wolf meet.

Jasmine sat with her head bent between her knees and felt the spirit of LaBoba. She knew her grandmother was trying to show her that if ever there was trouble in the land, she could seek her out in the inward soul of herself and there is where she'd find her answers.

Jasmine saw from the corner of her eye that her

grandmother was stirring. She whimpered, "Grandmother, oh, Grandmother, you've awakened."

Her grandmother opened her eyes but still had difficulty speaking. She weakly reached out and took Jasmine's hand into hers and moaned. Her long gray hair was stained with dried blood and lay matted to her scalp. Jasmine rubbed her grandmother's forehead where several bruises were, and then turned and fixed her eyes on the dreadfulness of the village and visualized what it had looked like before it was destroyed. Large statues had stood at the front entrance of the temple holding a golden egg and spear. It had given the village people a feeling of protection when returning from long journeys; now they were thrown to the ground and broken.

Jasmine's grandmother moaned again, and Jasmine looked back at her. "Oh Grandmother, I'm so glad you're alive. I don't know what I'd do without you. I still have so much to learn from you."

Her grandmother forced a smile and hoarsely whispered, "You have learned enough, granddaughter, but I shall not leave you; not yet. Jasmine, oh, how the village people fought to save the eggs, but the Vikons broke altars and took all the gold while they killed our people."

"I know Grandmother but lie still."

"Oh honey, I'll be fine, don't worry so about me."

"Okay Grandmother. I know you'll be fine because your strength will carry you through this unspeakable fright."

"Jasmine, many of the men ran away while the Vikons were killing and destroying our village. They wanted to warn you and the miners, but they are on foot and still lingering in the fields and forest."

Jasmine felt angry and vowed she'd avenge her parent's death. "Oh Grandmother, I will fight till the end to get our sacred golden eggs back. I'll go saddle Breezy and gather up the village people; the ones still alive. When I bring them back, together, we'll decide what to do."

"Good Jasmine! I have taught you well, and you have learned without fault. The miners should be back by dusk."

"Grandmother, when I meet up with the miners, we must call a council meeting, organized and appoint a group to go out and find the sacred eggs."

"Yes, granddaughter, that's what we'll do."

Jasmine looked toward where her grandmother's cottage once stood; burned to ashes and smoldering. As she turned around, she saw her grandmother's animals lying dead in the old corn field. She knew it was time to round up the villagers and take action.

She whistled and Breezy, her horse came running and then stood before her. She handed him an apple from her pocket and then climbed on him in search of villagers and when she found them, she cried out, "Come, my people, we must hasten. Time is short; there's no time to lose. Avenging our people's death and finding the golden eggs is now our main priority." She turned to her two brothers and said, "The miners are on their way here, go quickly and bring them back to the village."

After she finished gathering up all the surviving village people and after they rested for a while, she took them to her grandmother and saw that her brothers had returned with the miners. The men lifted her grandmother onto the wagon and then sat down around her discussing into the wee hours of the morning as to what they should do. They elected Jasmine's brother, Hardon, to become the new magistrate and they suggested Jasmine and her grandmother take their best warriors and go in search of the Vikons and retrieve the golden eggs.

Her grandmother, Ramara, told the villagers and Jasmine about Merrwin who lived a full three days away in a village called Gerhard Village, who was an old wizard and a spiritual healer and had more wisdom than anyone she knew. Ramara said Merrwin might be able to help guide her and Jasmine to find the golden eggs.

Charlotte Pattimari

Chapter Two ☼

In Search of the Sacred Golden Eggs

The next morning, Jasmine went to her grandmother and lingered over her for a few moments when she saw her sleeping on a bed of feathers. She then positioned herself next to her grandmother on the ground and thought about their journey together. Jasmine quickly moved slower when she noticed her grandmother had sat up and started rubbing her eyes.

"Grandmother, I worry about you going on this journey when you're not feeling well."

"Granddaughter, we have to get back our sacred eggs because they are important to our village. You will replace me soon and become the next shaman, and you've never been on a warrior trip, so I must go. This will likely be my last lesson for you."

"But Grandmother…"

"No, child, I shall go. You must do as a shaman would do and not allow your love for me to hold you back. Go, child. Go now so I can rest before we go."

"I will do as you say, Grandmother. I will be strong, and we'll go see Merrwin together."

Her grandmother reached in her pocket where she kept her precious stones, pulled out an old emerald one and handed it to Jasmine. "This stone belonged to my grandmother. Keep it close, Jasmine, and when you feel insecure about our journey, rub it because it will give you strength."

Jasmine took the stone and placed it in her pocket, then

thanked her grandmother.

The next morning, when the sun peeked over the mountains; in admiration, the men stopped and gazed in awe for a few minutes, and then went back to packing the wagon in preparation for their long journey. They loaded food, water, and other supplies they would need.

Jasmine gave a whistle to her beautiful black stallion, Breezy; immediately he came running with his long mane waving in the wind and stood before her. She knew he was her friend, and even as feisty as he was, he was loyal and very quick.

She handed him an apple and said, “Okay, Breezy, I know you like to take long rides down by the river's edge, but today we’re going on a long journey, and you must remain, my faithful friend, as you always have.”

She patted his head and wrapped her arms around his neck feeling pleased that he was going on the journey with her. After quickly saddling him up, she led him around the camp making sure everything was ready because she knew it was a long, dangerous three-day journey to Merrwin‘s castle. Only fifty warriors were going, but that’s all that was left after the village was burned to ashes with so many men destroyed, plus some had to remain to help Hardon rebuild the Sacred Temple.

Her brother, Hardon, the new magistrate, had mentioned something about people from other villages coming to help and for that she was relieved. She smiled thinly, her expression as grim as his, and said, “You know Hardon with this journey there may be many more men who will die before this war is over, but the root cause of it lies in our land and getting those golden eggs back so we can grow our food.”

Hardon sighed heavily. “I know Jasmine. I know. I wish you and grandmother well. I will go to the trees and whisper a prayer for your safe return home; hopefully with the golden eggs.” He gave her a long hug and said, “Goodbye, for now, Jasmine; be safe.”

The warriors lifted Jasmine's grandmother onto the wagon along with the other men and the wagon pulled out with Jasmine riding on Breezy beside them. Jazzel, Cosmos, and Philo poked their heads out of Jasmine's pouch as they made clicking noises. She laughed and said, "Okay ferrets behave; we're on our way."

Jasmine looked back as they pulled out and noticed snow on the ground and felt a bit chilled by the coldness. She pulled her buffalo coat closer to her chest and sighed as she looked over at her grandmother bundled up with her bear blanket.

They traveled most of the day, and everyone was weary and tired, so before it started getting dark, they stopped. The men set up camp for the night near the big boulders.

Jasmine removed Breezy's saddle and said, "Now, don't go far Breezy because I'm not tying you up."

All settled in for the night, the men lighted a warm fire while Jasmine and her grandmother moved near the warmth. Jasmine did a meditation on her grandmother for her body to heal quickly. Then they settled back and began talking about their first day's journey. Both were pleased they hadn't run into any Vikons and hoped the next day would go well. During the night they heard animal sounds but felt safe as they drifted off to sleep. Jasmine rubbed her stone and closed her eyes. Shortly after, she heard Breezy snorting and kicking at the dirt she moved over to see what was upsetting her and saw a small bird that had fallen out of its nest hoppling along and couldn't seem to fly. Jasmine picked it up and right away noticed its wing had been hurt so she carried it back to her bedside, and tucked it beside her blanket, thinking she'd repair it in the morning, and take it with them on their journey.

The next morning camp broke up and soon after headed to their destination. After several miles, they saw a small farm dwelling, and as they neared, they heard a woman screaming. Quickly riding to the back of the dwelling, they saw five Vikons holding a woman while her husband laid across a pile of wood where he had been beaten to death. Over near the home, a Vikon held her two children with his sword to their throats.

Jasmine's men looked around and saw about ten Vikons, so she ordered the men to stop the Vikons. They jumped off their horses and ran with their swords drawn to fight them off. Some Vikons ran off while the others were being killed by Jasmine's men. The man with the children grabbed one under each arm and began running. Jasmine's grandmother leaped from the wagon and headed toward the men with Jasmine running behind her.

All of a sudden, her grandmother stopped in her tracks. She held out her arms and the white spirit of a wolf came out of her chest and leaped onto the Vikon holding the children. The great white spirit wolf ripped at his neck, and he immediately released the children and Jasmine ran over and grabbed them soon after the Vikon fell to the ground while he slowly closed his eyes, forever.

The children pulled loose from Jasmine and ran to their mother. They grabbed onto her legs while Jasmine's grandmother stretched out her arms and the white spirit wolf faded away as her grandmother's form reappeared.

Jasmine looked at her grandmother in shock and then cried, "Oh, Grandmother! Oh, I didn't know you could do that." "

"Jasmine, remember the story I told you about; the old woman, Laboba?"

"Yes, Grandmother, I do."

"Well, granddaughter, all you have to do is ask for help, and the white spirited wolf appears."

The mother of the children dropped to her knees trembling violently while resting her face on her children's back. It was a kind of release. Jasmine looked over at the woman and her children, and then walked over and asked, "Are you alright?"

The woman gasped hoarsely for breath, trying to hold back sobs while rocking gently back and forth holding tightly onto to her children. "A Vikon held me and wouldn't let me go to my husband. I wiggled away, but he caught me. I bit his arm, and he kicked me, but I got free and ran across the muddy, torn up fields rattling through dried stalks of corn, and that's where he caught me again and had his way. Only then did I realize my frantically appalling predicament. I thought he was going to kill me."

"Are your children alright?"

She released her children and stood up and said, "Oh yes, they are; thanks to you. They could have been killed."

Jasmine stood stunned by it all and now realized why the story her grandmother had told her about Laboba was her favorite, but never in a million years did she know the white spirit wolf could jump out of her grandmother. She wondered if she could call it out as her grandmother had. She remembered her grandmother telling her it was inside of her. With a half cry of anguish, she walked toward her horse and noticed Cosmos was running around on the ground picking up spilled coins and laying them in the wagon which changed her anger to laughter.

After the mother walked back to the house with her children, Jasmine's grandmother caught up with her and said, "Always remember Jasmine what I said to you and what you just saw. You are capable of the same."

"Oh grandmother, you are so wise, but I don't know if I could draw the white spirited wolf out of me."

"Granddaughter, when the time comes, you will. Now you must believe this and stop doubting yourself because you are to take my place when it is time. You must be strong."

"I will try grandmother."

After the commotion settled down, Jasmine's men buried the dead woman's husband along with the dead Vikons.

"We must go now Jasmine," said her grandmother. "My instincts tell me that the Vikons will return with more men, so we'd better load up the woman and her children. We will take them with us."

Soon after eating and loading everything back into the wagon, they headed back on their journey to see Merrwin.

After many miles, they came across a crystal-clear stream and decided to stop and bath and set up camp for the night. The group sat around the campfire talking about the farmhouse and all that had happened. The children were in the wagon tucked under the bear blanket fast asleep, and the little bird with the fixed wing was sitting near them chirping.

After all the chatter had stopped, everyone went to their own bed while two guards stayed up and kept an eye on the camp. By early morning both men were so exhausted, they climbed on the wagon and fell into a deep sleep.

Jasmine said, "Grandmother, I feel the Vikons are coming soon and bringing an army with them. We should pack up and leave."

"Granddaughter, you are already showing your instincts are alive. Yes, I too, feel it; we should go. We can eat while we travel."

Jasmine squeezed her emerald stone tightly in her hand and secured the pouch tightly over her shoulder.

Within a few miles of Merrwin's castle, Jasmine could see that her grandmother was uneasy. The ferrets began moving around inside the leather bag, and Jasmine said, "Hey, hold it down in there!" And just after scolding the ferrets, the wounded baby bird flew over their heads. "Oh, baby bird, you've flown away. What is going on? Everyone seems uneasy."

Jazzell climbed out of the bag and wrapped his body close to Jasmine's arm, making it look like a buddle of fur. "Okay, now that you're comfortable, perhaps you'll calm down." Jasmine chuckled.

Soon after, they entered the large wooden gate leading up to the castle's front entrance. The castle's head servant stepped out the big doors and asked, "To whom shall I tell Lord

Merrwin is calling?"

"Tell her it is Ramara, of the Valley of the Yellow Stones with her granddaughter, Jasmine."

The castle's servant wearing his white and gold robe requested they follow him. Jasmine's men and the little family were escorted to a side door where they were served a cool drink and hot meal while Jasmine and her grandmother went into the setting-room to wait for Merrwin. Shortly after, the castle servant brought in tea for the two.

Co-author Donnie

Co-author Melissa

Chapter Three ☼

A Visit to Merrwin and Bevin, Lady of Lake Isabella

Ramara and Jasmine were drinking tea when Merrwin stepped into the study. Ramara immediately stood up and greeted her old friend and then they embraced. “It’s been far too long my friend.”

“Yes, it has Ramara. What brings you here?”

“We shall discuss it Merrwin.”

Ramara looked over at Jasmine and said, “This is Jasmine, my granddaughter, the next shaman.”

“Haunting Ramara, she looks just like you when we first met.”

“So, I’ve been told,” answered Ramara. She set her empty cup on the table and then began telling Merrwin the story about the Vikons and the golden eggs they stole. She proceeded on about the farmer who was killed and how they had brought his wife and children with them.

“Very well, the little family will stay among my people. Now, let me tell you Ramara, the Vikons’ are beginning to come around with their killing spirit more and more.” Merrwin said as she gestured to the servant for more tea by holding her empty cup up in the air.

Ramara grimaced as she shook her head. “They must be stopped, but for now we need to concentrate on our sacred golden eggs. It is important for all surrounding villages.”

“Yes, they must be, Ramara. I saw you coming in the fire. I say to you from my faithful intuition that you must go to Bevin, Lady of Lake Isabella. Now, remember this old friend when you get there you will think you are looking at a lake, but in reality, it's her castle. She has it hidden so the unknowns cannot find her." Merrwin said while the servant filled her cup up.

"I will go," Ramara said.

"Grandmother, we must get some rest before going."

"Yes, Granddaughter, we shall."

Merrwin shook her head, yes. "Now, Ramara, when you get there, you will stand on the shore and tell Bevin that I've sent you. I will go to my magic fire and alert her to your coming."

"Grandmother knew you would be able to help us Merrwin."

"Yes child, I will help you, in fact I have something for you to take on your journey, but for now you need to rest then you will leave tomorrow at the first sun."

"Thank you Merrwin. I *am* tired."

Ramara said, "Merrwin, you are most kind."

Merrwin stood up and said, "You both sleep while my servants prepare a feast for you. We shall eat in the dining room tonight and light ten candles for your safety."

After a peaceful rest, Ramara and Jasmine joined Merrwin at her long wooden table and immediately saw five candles flaming. Merrwin stood up and said, "Please, Ramara you light two candles to make your trip a safe one."

Ramara took the candle torch and lit two candles while saying, "This is for us to have a safe trip."

Jasmine accepted the torch from her grandmother and lit two candles while Merrwin lit the last one. They both said in unison, "This is for a safe trip."

The candle danced in its flame, and Jasmine smiled as she rubbed her stone.

The castle's head servant came in and lighted all the candles in the square glass jars hanging from the ceiling while the servants carried platters of hot steaming food. Jasmine eyed the platter of shrimp with a golden buttery sauce over the top. She could hardly wait to sink her teeth into them. Her ferret moved and positioned himself better around her neck, and she chuckled at his fur tickling her.

More platters arrived with layers and layers of hot steaming food sending its aroma throughout the room. Fresh spices were placed over the tops of them, and everyone was eager to eat. Shortly after the servants filled their plates, two dancing girls came in and started dancing around the room. That is when the lighter conversation began.

Ramara and Merrwin told Jasmine old childhood stories of how they played together in the village and played down by the river's edge. Each story brought laughter to the table and Jasmine giggled in the excitement. It was good hearing her grandmother's happy laughter in a way Jasmine had not seen in a while.

Before the tables were cleared and wine served, Merrwin handed Jasmine a small band to go around her head and told her to wear it in battle for it would protect her. It was silver with shiny crystals attached to it and as she placed it on her head, it sparkled and sent out flashes of light that made a humming sound. Jasmine removed the band noticing it folded up and easily fit into her pouch.

After another hour of enjoyable reminiscing, they retired to a good night sleep for their next morning's journey.

At the arrival of the first sun, they bid their farewells and left the castle's safety and Merrwin's caring friendship. The snow had stopped, and it was beginning to warm up a bit. Jasmine's two ferrets were starting to get restless, so they stopped and let them run and play on the dry ground. Philo crawled out of the leather pouch and scrambled down inside Jasmine's shirt and tickled her. Jasmine started to squirm and giggle as she reached in and pulled him out and said, "Philo, behave and get down on the ground and play awhile. We are only here for a moment; jump down and play."

Soon as they arrived at the lake's edge facing the north, Jasmine and Ramara stood at the shore, and Jasmine bellowed out, “Bevin! Lady of Lake Isabella! It’s Ramara, and Jasmine sent here by Merrwin. She said you would be expecting us.”

After waiting for a few minutes and still no response, they wondered if they had come to the wrong place. All at once, the ground began shaking and there stood before them a long wooden bridge which led to the castle’s entrance. Jasmine rode ahead of the group feeling eerie realizing the lake had turned into a castle. Jasmine looked back at the men and saw that they were approaching with her grandmother sitting up tall in the wagon. She could see that Ramara looked excited as the bridge disappeared and again became the lake. Jasmine entered the castle with the men right behind her and almost immediately Bevin came out to greet them. She was beautiful with her long curly brown hair that went all the way to her waist. Her eyes were a sparkling gray that had spots of yellow in them. She wore a long golden robe that glittered as she walked toward them. She walked with class with her shoulders back and her face proud. She was well over 6 feet tall and looked like a goddess.

“I’ve been expecting you. Welcome! Please follow me.”

Jasmine and Ramara followed with the men behind them. As soon as they entered into a room filled with armor, Ramara gasped, and Jasmine looked at Bevin and said, “You have enough armor here to make this whole nation safe, Lady of Lake Isabella.”

“Yes, it is most important to have enough. Please have a seat, and I will have some food prepared for you. Ramara got up from her chair and moved over to a wall of swords, gently touching a few and right away began feeling full of energy. She pulled her hand back quickly and wondered if it was her own excitement or if the swords were filling her with energy.

Within the hour the servants brought food in to them and as they all sit around the big rock table Bevin began telling how the castle was an illusion of a lake because it brought great safety to the land.

"This illusion has been here for ages and formed by other castle holders before us. A great spell was cast on the castle to hide her land intruders. Back then, wars were a daily event and since this castle holds many magical things, it had to be protected." Bevin said and then motioned for Jasmine to follow her. "I have something for you to help you find what you are seeking."

"Thank you, Bevin, Merrwin said you could help us and would give me a gift."

"Yes, Merrwin, as always is correct," Bevin said as she picked up a gold sword that had jewels seeded in the sword's handle. "This is a magical sword in which you will win every fight you encounter. It will help you find the sacred eggs. This sword is made of the same material as your golden eggs, except it is for triumphant instead of counting time and precession of the Equinox."

"Thank you, Bevin. You are most helpful, and we will always credit you with our love and good weather."

Ramara stepped forward and touched the sword and said, "My granddaughter will use this well."

"Yes Ramara, I know she is going to be the next shaman, and this magical sword will keep her safe and release its magical powers whenever needed. It's hers as long as she uses it wisely and continues to have a pure heart. I warn you that the moment her heart is no longer pure it will disappear into the hands of the next pure heart."

"We understand Bevin. It's like this magical castle. All things work for those of good will."

"Yes, you understand it well, Ramara." Bevin said and then turned to Jasmine." Jasmine, the Vikons are on the side of the tallest mountain near the northeast side. You follow the trail, and with you, I will send fifty of my strongest soldiers. They know what to do in battles and how to keep you safe. Later, if need be, we'll send out more. Merrwin will alert me with her fire signs. Meditate for a while, and then you must go."

When the men went to load up the wagon and feed the horses, they saw food, water, and supplies had been placed on the wagon and horses for their long journey ahead.

Jasmine sent out a whistle, and without delay Breezy came running and stood in front of her. She quickly placed an apple in his mouth and said, “We have a long journey ahead Breezy; eat this for your strength.”

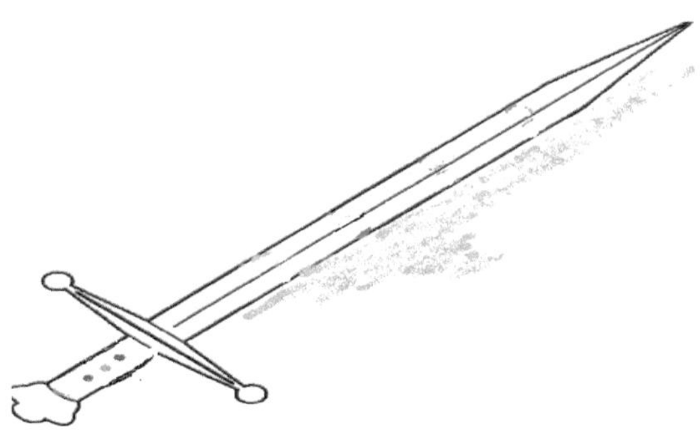

Magical sword from Lady of the Lake

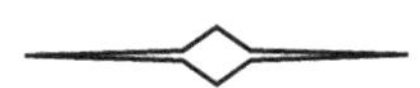

Chapter Four ☼
Ivan

Feeling depressed over the sudden death of his wife, Sir Ivan was wondering through the forest trying to get past his emotional pain. It had been several months, but it didn't matter to him because it seemed like yesterday. He had left his farm he and his brother shared, which set outside a small town called, Brasco, ten miles north of Valley of the Yellow Stones. He left because he could no longer tolerate the farm without his wife, but today he was reminiscing about her softness and how happy they had been together when suddenly, he heard a loud roaring. Ivan hurried toward the noise and saw an unsightly dragon attacking a white lion. Ivan stayed on his horse and attacked the dragon. He drew his sword high in the air and came down hard on the dragon's neck while the white lion attacked the dragon's tail with his teeth, biting him hard and fast. The dragon flipped his tail up and down, throwing the lion sideways and then up, but the lion hung on and kept biting the dragon's tail as Ivan continued to hit the dragon's neck with his sword until the dragon fell to the ground, dead. After the long struggle ended, Ivan said, "White Lion, that's what I shall call you from now on." The lion was so grateful for Ivan's help and saving his life that he began following him where ever he went. Ivan grew accustomed to the following

lion and it soon became his good companion. White Lion killed wild game for the knight and Ivan and would fetch them water. They'd lie near a fire with Ivan's head on the lion's back and sleep the night away.

A few days later, Ivan met Ruthus, Lady of the Fountain, who was sitting near the fountain, crying.

"What is the matter with you, who cries at the fountain?" Ivan said as he got off his horse and walked over to her.

Ruthus looked up as the tears streamed down her cheeks, and said, "I gave bad advice to the town magistrate's servant, and now he wants to charge me with treason."

"Where may I ask is the guard?" Ivan asked.

"Why he's standing over near the red wall," Ruthus said as she pointed in the direction of the wall.

Ivan walked over to the guard and defended the lady by saying he would speak to the town's magistrate by noon tomorrow. He couldn't allow her to be put to death or burned at the stake as she feared.

Ivan went to the next town to seek lodging when he discovered a fairly destroyed town. He asked questions and was told a giant named Binar of the mountain had killed the Lord's three sons and threatened to kill his other four sons if the lord didn't deliver his daughter to him. Right away Ivan promised to face the giant early the next morning. He knew he had to defend Ruthus by noon and luckily the next morning the giant arrived several hours before noon.

Without delay, Ivan challenged and began to attack the giant, Binar. He drew his sword and plunged the blade into the giant's leg. This made Binar so upset that he picked Ivan up and threw him into the water trough. He jumped up, soaked, and ran back to the giant and again drew his sword and this time he cut off one of his toes. The giant screamed and then in his pain and anger reached for Ivan with fire coming out of his eyes. White Lion saw the look in Binar's eyes and leaped at him and began biting his neck while Ivan attacked his leg. The giant fell to the ground with his neck bleeding profusely, but White Lion continued to bite until the giant's movement ceased and his eyes closed. After it was over, and the giant composed himself, he shouted for all the town's people to hear that it was unfair, and that Ivan would have to fight him again in order to save the Lord's daughter. Ivan agreed and had the lion confined to the castle. The giant gained the upper hand in combat and Ivan was losing. White Lion knew that Ivan was losing, so he jumped to the low wall and leaped over it and flew through the air onto Binar and locked on his neck while Ivan recovered and threw his sword right into the giant's heart; Binar dropped to his knees. As Ivan was thanking White Lion, the light left the giant's eyes. Ivan and White Lion walked away.

The sons of the lord were released, and the Lord told Ivan he would always have a place in his kingdom. Ivan thanked the Lord and went on his way. He feared he didn't have time to keep his appointment with the Magistrate, Swantis, but arrived right at noon and defended Ruthus, the Keeper of the Fountain. Ivan used his common sense by saying that it was wrong to charge Ruthus with treason when she was only trying to help. Ivan said, "If you charge her with treason, who then will offer you advice? And if there is a next one, will she fear offering you bad advice, therefore not giving you any advice at all?"

"You speak well knight, or shall I call you a farmer? I have heard of your insight into these strong matters. I shall release Ruthus. I shall listen to your advice; not because I was wrong

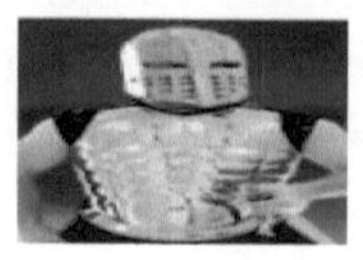

in charging her with treason, but because you offer perfect wisdom in this matter."

Queen Claudine had been listening to the challenge Ivan had given the Magistrate Swantis and became immediately impressed. She requested that Ruthus, the Keeper of the Fountain, to serve as her companion. Ruthus accepted the Queen's request, and as she walked away, she turned and asked Ivan who he was.

"Why, I'm King of the White Lion."

Ivan jumped on Gallo and soon after left and went back to the Forest, and as he was wandering along, he happened upon Jasmine and her grandmother. The knight's eyes lit up as he looked upon such beauty, but a powerful strength as shown in her eyes. He quickly introduced himself to Jasmine and her grandmother, "I am Sir Ivan at your service," he said with his brown eyes sparkling and his heart pounding against his chest. He then tipped his head in a bow.

Jasmine said, "It's my pleasure to meet you Sir Ivan, my grandmother and I are on a mission to save the Sacred Golden Eggs for our village."

Sir Ivan said, "I've heard about your mission. I'm at your service, that is, if you call upon me to do so."

Ramara noticed how handsome the knight was with his tall, slender figure, tanned smooth skin, and the kindest smile she liked. She thought he would be perfect for Jasmine but observed Jasmine hadn't shown any interest because she had other things on her mind. Sir Ivan said he knew of a camp up ahead where they could settle in for the night and since everyone was exhausted and needed rest they headed to his suggested destination.

After resting and discussing with Sir Ivan about joining them on their search, Ramara and Jasmine were delighted to have him traveling across the mountains in search of the golden eggs. Not long on the road, they came across a place where women were being driven out from their town.

Ramara questioned the town's people, "What's going on here? Why are you forcing your women to leave?"

Not a soul spoke but continued to use whips to beat down on the backs of the women while they left the town in groups. Jasmine ran into the town's hall to seek out the King of Shad and that's where she learned that two sprites had forced the King of Shad to give up forty maidens each year for sparing the king's life. He continued to say that the maidens were to live a life as servants eating little food with no payment for their labor.

Earlier the next morning Ivan rushed up to Jasmine to request her help. "We must rescue them from this immoral custom. I know of this King and he will listen if we offer to rid him of these two sprites."

Jasmine picked up her sword and walked with Ivan into the Lord's chambers and afterward left and went to the maidens and told them that they would rescue them from the sprites and not to worry.

"We will help put an end to this disgusting custom." Ivan called out to the women.

Jasmine and Ivan hurried to the king's castle and demanded to see King Shad. Jasmine lifted her magical sword and they were allowed in.

"What is so urgent that you would draw your sword on my men?" The king angrily shouted.

Ivan stepped forward and said, "King Shad, please forgive us for being so harsh with your men. We know you are a good King and will forgive us if you'll hear the reason we are here."

" Very well, speak." King Shad spoke with a calmer voice.

"King Shad, we are here to offer you assistance with this custom of taking women out of your town. We know they have threatened your life if you don't allow forty women to be taken each year, and also know you have lost a lot of your army. We have warriors that will stop this. Just say the word."

"I say, full force ahead! I will honor your offer. Now, go and bring on your warriors and end this custom," King Shad said.

Jasmine went back to where her grandmother and men had set up camp and told them to settle in for another night because she was going to tend to a few things before journeying on, but she'd be back by morning. She then went back to Ivan and without delay left with fifty men on the mountain outside of town where there was a small village. Jasmine with her magic sword called out the sprites, but they refused to come out or fight. Ivan had been told they had lions that were on the mad side and would attack without warning. So, he had White Lion befriend the golden lion who was the leader and White Lion and the golden lion lead the lions into a room made of stone where they couldn't attack. The sprites saw what they were doing and became angry and started attacking Ivan and Jasmine. The two of them stood back to back and fought hard. With her magical sword Jasmine raised it high and many of the sprites ran to hide. She lifted her sword toward the stone room where the lions were and said, "Come out, break down the stone wall and attack the sprites."

The lions broke down the door and started to attack one of the sprites. One lion set his teeth into the sprite's neck until he fell to the ground, dead. Jasmine lifted her sword and it struck another, sending him to darkness. The remaining sprites pleaded for mercy, promising to end the custom.

"Show us your word is good. Release the maidens!" Ivan yelled out to the sprites. They were released immediately, and Jasmine and Ivan walked away with Jasmine lifting her sword only one more time at the sprites. The jewels on the handle lighted up and the sprites cowered back and fell to the ground pleading, "Don't hurt us."

Jasmine and Ivan were tired but felt splendid about victoriously winning the battle and fighting back to back with one another. Sir Ivan looked over at White Lion and saw that he was standing near the golden lion he had befriended. He chuckled as he and Jasmine went back to tell King Shad the good news.

King Shad was grateful and invited them to stay and live in his town and become part of the town's counsel, but Jasmine told the king they had to find the golden eggs.

"Well, in that case, I'll send fifty of my best men with you as my thanks to you for helping rid us of the sprites."

Jasmine was pleased and thanked the King. Ivan decided to go off into the forest and spend some time recuperating from his fierce fighting. He told Jasmine he'd return and help her find the golden eggs in a couple of days. Jasmine returned back to her grandmother, Ramara, and told her about the battle with the sprites.

"Jasmine, you're going to be a good shaman. I'm proud of you."

Chapter Five ☼

War at Galt

"Come on, Gallo," Ivan said to his horse. He jumped up on him, and off they went to the path leading toward the forest with White Lion walking along beside them, and behind him walking his good friend, Golden Lion. They had gone some miles, and the road was running down a slope into the forest when Ivan realized he wasn't feeling that awful heavy loss, he had felt a couple of days ago. Today, his mind was on Jasmine and how she had fought back to back with him. She was an excellent sword's woman, yet all the while remaining a beautiful woman. His heart fluttered as he thought about her smiling up at him with her pale blue eyes after the battle had been won. He didn't feel connected to the loneliness of the forest anymore, but he knew he needed rest before catching up with Jasmine and her grandmother, so he decided to set up camp and stretch out for the night. He knew the golden eggs were important for her village and he'd fight to get them back, but for now, he needed to see his old friend, Marcus, and get the white Arabian horse he offered. He boasted it would outrun any Vikon horse.

Jasmine knew she had to find the Vikons and get the golden eggs back for her village, but she also knew she had to rest before continuing her journey. She reflected back to the energy she had felt while fighting beside Ivan. She grinned, knowing the maidens were freed because of them. She hadn't realized at the time of parting, but she now knew she had wanted to go with Ivan to the ends of the earth after their fierce battle. Yet she had responsibilities and needed to stay on her journey and find the golden eggs for her village. She was thankful for the many men that had been given to her for the cause, and yet she knew she had to have many more in order to defeat the Vikons.

After resting for several hours, her grandmother came to her and said they must leave. She jerked awake and followed her grandmother to her horse and noticed her grandmother had climbed up on a white Arabian horse. She looked smug with her hands on her hips and said, "well, granddaughter, let's get on our way. We have wars to fight and golden eggs to collect."

All of a sudden Jasmine's little Cosmos ferret ran as fast as he could, jumped up on the horse next to Ramara and pulled her hat off her head and threw it on the ground. He snuggled up to Ramara and settled in. "Well, what have we here little Cosmos? Are you trying to tell me you want to ride with me?"

Jasmine chuckled and said, "Okay Cosmos, go ahead and ride with grandmother. By the way, where did you get that horse, Grandmother?"

"Sir Ivan brought it by and said he'd catch up with us at the sign of the next sunrise; on the trail to Galt."

"Oh, he did, did he?" Jasmine smiled as she pulled the reins on her horse and led him beside the wagon. Soon after, all 150 men followed behind Jasmine and her grandmother.

The ride was grimy and exhausting with the sun climbing to the peak of the mountains, and the mist in the valley below thinned out. The last of them were floating away, just overhead, as curls of white clouds surged on the stiffening breeze from the East that was now flickering and moving the tree limbs. A long way down in the valley-bottom were Vikon warriors, drinking and carrying on near a fire in their drunkenness. The small river could now be seen as they approached around the East side of the mountain.

Just as Jasmine, Ramara and their army entered the road leading to the kingdom of Galt, Ivan galloped up beside Jasmine and said, "Shall we stop over near the aged trees and discuss our plan before entering into Galt?"

Jasmine smiled over at Ivan and then nodded and turned her reins for Breezy to go near the trees. "How did you know about Galt?"

Ivan grinned and then said, "I have my ways."

The men unloaded food while Ivan started a campfire. During dinner, they discussed how they were going to approach the Vikons and get back the eggs. After the meeting, Ivan stood and looked over the land. He could see all the Galt's farmsteads and little stockades, barns, and fields, but nowhere could he see any Vikons or movement. Many pathways across the jade fields were much coming and going; wagons moving in two lines of positions towards the Noble Wall. Now and again, a horseman rode up with a large wooden crate filled with something, dropping it off then returning for another. Ivan couldn't figure out from the distance what the painting was on the boxes, but he guessed it was either food or seed for the fields. He turned back around and noticed the wagon and horses were packed and ready for them to continue their journey. They traveled another mile when they entered into Galt and immediately saw Lord Galt's castle. The men entered the great Hall of Galt while Jasmine and Ramara went to meet with the king. Ivan stayed behind to keep an eye on the Vikon armies down deeper in the valley, getting drunk out by the big oak trees.

Right away Jasmine could see the castle was built well as she passed through the long halls leading to the King's Chief Room. The stones were big with red and yellow colors holding strong to the walls; stout enough to hold an army of men without any problems. Ramara took in a deep breath and whispered, "Jasmine, promise me, if there's any trouble, you'll run as fast as you can to get out of here. Do not try to save me."

"Grandmother, what are you trying to say? Did you have a vision?"

"No granddaughter. No vision, but my intuition is feeling

mighty strange."

"Grandmother, I cannot leave you."

"Jasmine promise me. You are to be the next shaman and must promise me."

"Grandmother!"

"Promise me Granddaughter."

"Okay Grandmother, I promise."

As Jasmine and Ramara stepped into the room where the King was, his guard gestured with this brass pole for them to be seated in front of the king. They sat down on a bear rug and waited for the King to speak and when he did, Ramara said, "King of the Galts, I've traveled for a full day to see you. I know your father was a good man and would be terribly upset by what the Vikon armies are doing."

The King frowned. "What may I ask are they doing?"

"They are taking women and using them, killing their husbands for entertainment, stealing children, and burning down villages," Ivan said.

"They also took our Sacred Golden Eggs from the Valley of the Yellow Stones, and as your father knew these eggs are for all the lands near and far; not Valley of the Yellow Stones alone," Jasmine said.

The king looked at his guard and told him to put his brass pole down and then said, "I'm not aware of these happenings, but I will help with any need you may have. I will offer you my army to get the sacred golden eggs back."

The king's servant appeared at the door of the room and bellowed out,

"My Lord I'm most sorry to disturb you, but there is an army of Vikons coming this way."

The King stood up and stormed back at his servant, "call the town's people to come to the castle grounds and tell them to prepare for battle. Inform the captain and army immediately. This is going to be a bloody day!"

Ivan ran to the guard tower and saw the mass of Vikons

approaching the castle. The King standing beside him shouted, "Open the gate!"

The gate was opened, and the captain positioned his men "Get ready for attack. Steady your hands for we shall wait until they get closer," the captain yelled as the gate closed behind them.

Jasmine ran to the castle's door and raised her sword as Ivan stood behind her waiting for anyone who dared to come through the door.

Drums rolled, and fires leaped up while men fought and killed; both Vikons and Galt warriors. Ramara ran to the opening in a small door and raised her sword and brought it down hard on each head that tried to enter the door. She screamed and kicked them aside and raised her sword for another and another until Ivan stepped over and took her position while she stood in the darkness of the room to regroup herself. She poured water over her head from the King's pitcher and then set it down just in time to raise her sword to prevent a Vikon from striking the king. One Vikon hit her hard on the shoulder and she fell to the floor as Jasmine held her sword high over the man's head. The handle's jewels began to sparkle and sent out fire to his head and it instantly turned him into ashes.

With a lasting despairing effort, Ramara raised herself on her hands and struggled until she lifted herself up and fell into Ivan's arms. He carried her over to the bear rug and gently laid her down. She moaned as Jasmine wrapped her shoulder with the material of the hanging cloth lying over the King's throne. She fell back into exhaustion and motioned for Jasmine to leave her. "Go, Granddaughter. Go help the men!"

Dazed as she was with pain and weariness, she dragged herself over to the water basin and looked down into the water, mirroring a glimpse of what was happening in the future. What she saw turned her face white, and Jasmine ran over to her and said, "what is it, Grandmother?"

"Nothing we can't handle granddaughter. Go back! Leave me!" Ramara didn't want to frighten Jasmine, so she kept her vision to herself and dragged herself over to the hot coals the King had burning in his pit and threw in a piece of her cloth and as the flames came up, she chanted, *fire, fire rise up and transpire Consa, the gatekeeper. I need her,"* up from the flames rose Consa. "Consa, my heart sings with the sight of you."

"Ramara, what is your need?"

"Consa, we need your help, we are out-numbered by the Vikons. I need you to bring an army of the ancient ones." Ramara moaned in her pained spirit. "I'm weak, but my spirit is strong. Send the ancient ones!"

"Fear not Ramara. The ancient ones will come within the hour. Hold on until then." Consa said as she began to fade out into a smoky cloud.

The captain started dropping rocks from the towers and hot oil. The army began throwing hot coals with shovels as the Vikons placed long ladders up against the walls and began climbing up. The king's men were shooting arrows and throwing spears. At the front entrance, the Vikons were trying to break down the castle door with heavy logs. Jasmine lifted her sword as they finally broke down the door and began running in. The jewels started to sparkle and sent out flames as the Vikons entered, turning them instantly into ashes. From the small door of the King's Chief room, the Vikons were entering, and one hit the king on the head while another ran toward Ivan. Jasmine lifted her sword toward him, and he fell down into a pile of ashes. Ivan tore off his shirt and wrapped the king's head and then swung his sword and a Vikon fell to the ground, dead.

Chapter Six

Jasmine and Ivan

Everything was happening fierce and fast, and it took the entire King's men, and Jasmine with her sword to keep the Vikon's away. Ivan was tending to the king, making sure he was all right. He held his head up, to sip on water, he had scooped up in his hand. Cosmo was hiding under a cart trying to stay out of the way. Breezy was nervous and pacing back and forth until she finally panicked and jumped over the wall into the king's courtyard, and began standing on her hind legs, trampling Vikons' as she came down on their bodies. Ivan's White Lion was jumping on Vikons' and biting their necks until they fell to the ground.

In the distance, Ramara heard a horn, and then Consa appeared with Akish her guard lion at her side. She appeared before Ramara and blew her small horn, and all the armies she summoned were high on the hill looking down at the Vikons. When they heard the horn, hundreds began running down the hillsides attacking Vikons. One by one Vikon's fell to the ground. Jasmine stood in the castle's tower and looked out over the land and saw nothing but bodies lying on the ground.

Sir Ivan had placed King Galt near Ramara and jumped down the wall with his rope and began fighting Vikons on the bridge and throwing them off as fast as he could.

Jasmine with her magic sword was fighting each Vikon that entered through the King's side door. The castle's grounds were a gory disaster with fire everywhere and before long what Vikons were left ran off into the night.

Finally, the courtyard became calm. Hundreds of men were lying on the ground, and some of King Galt's men were sitting on the stone walls with their heads down and their swords lying beside them. King Galt stood up in pain and looked down on his courtyard, seeing death everywhere. He motioned for his army to return back and clean up the brutal catastrophe. "Bury the men, including the Vikons!" He yelled and then turned to Ivan and said, "You are always welcome in my kingdom, as are Jasmine and Ramara. Consa, without you, we might not have won this war. I invite you all to return to my kingdom and celebrate our victory."

By the next morning Ramara's men loaded up the wagon and horses, and as Jasmine got on Breezy with her ferrets, she turned back to look at her grandmother on the wagon smiling but still in pain from the hit on the shoulder. As soon as they reached camp, Jasmine would do a meditative healing on her grandmother, but for now, she knew it was important to get the wounded and tired men to camp where they could rest and receive treatment.

She waved to King Galt and smiled over at Ivan who rode his horse beside her. They galloped out of the land of the Galt's, heading back down the mountain to regroup before going on ahead to search for their Sacred Golden Eggs. Armies were following; hundreds of men hungry and in need of rest. Consa had promised to send over food and water. Bevin of Lake Isabella also said she would address all of her men to rescue the eggs and to bring food and wine. She said it was time to regroup with a celebration.

As they neared the campsite where they were going to spend a couple of days resting, Jasmine looked over at Ivan and said, "We've won another battle, Ivan."

Ivan moved his horse up close to Jasmine and reached out and touched her hand and winked. "Your grandmother is right;

you *will* make a great shaman Jasmine. After we rest and celebrate, I'll go with you to find the golden eggs."

Jasmine smiled as she galloped away and headed to the campsite. Ramara looked back as the wagon moved farther away and saw vultures flying over making a squawking sound as if to say the fighting is over.

Soon after arriving, the men unloaded and set up camp, and then they leaned back; for a moment they bent their heads down and did not speak while Jasmine did a healing for her grandmother. Then suddenly Ramara sat up and threw another log into the fire and said, "This is for all those that died in the battle. Wars are not a happy thing, but they must go on as long as there are those who think they own all of the land."

Jasmine looked up and saw a falling star and pointed to Ivan, "look."

He squeezed her hand, brought it up to his lips and then responded to Ramara, "Nevertheless, I, who have been called the great 'warrior in battle' dislike any thought of war. Knowing it is something I cannot escape is poorer than poor."

"What a warring day it has been, and my greatest hope is that we find the golden eggs and live in peace from here on out," Jasmine said as she put her hand on her ferret cuddling close to her shoulder. Lately, it seemed to be his favorite spot.

"That would be good, Jasmine. Perhaps you will visit my farm one day, that is, once this is over." Ivan closed his eyes and reflected what it would be like having Jasmine living on his farm.

The next morning, Consa, true to her word, sent over a feast for the men and a magic ring for Jasmine. She looked down at her ring and remembered the message Consa had sent; the ring would make her disappear and appear wherever she wanted if while rubbing the ring she directed her thoughts to the destination. Jasmine knew she would use it wisely as Consa had requested.

As Consa's people began unloading boxes the men yelled

out with glee and started to set up tables made of old dead tree trunks while Ivan laid pieces of wooden material over the top and Consa's people began filling the table with platters of fruit, toasted wild game and platters of steaming roasted bread. When the wine was placed on the table, the men hollered with pleasure. Ramara began pouring it into wooden cups and then the dancing started. Ivan looked full into Jasmine's eyes and offered her his hand. She took it and they began dancing around the fire. The men whooped and hollered when they stopped and stood gazing into one another's eyes, Ivan realized his tiredness had left him and he wanted to run to the fields with Jasmine, fall in the grass and put his lips to hers, but he retained himself because he knew that would have to be after the golden eggs were found. He turned and walked over to the log and sat down. Jasmine looked puzzled at his reactions and wondered what she had done to cause him to turn away.

Ivan remembered that feminine smell; the fragrance of Itel, his deceased wife. The scent had carried him back to the days when he and she ran and played in the fields, falling to the ground laughing. Jasmine looked into his eyes, but he was in pain and had to look away. She jerked her body around and went over to the table and snatched up a berry and threw it into her mouth then swallowed the last drop of her wine and poured more. Ivan knew he had hurt her feelings, so he walked over to her and pulled her to his chest and kissed her hard and fast, then released her and said, "Stop drinking! A time will come for us, Jasmine."

Jasmine flipped around and stormed over to Breezy, jumped on him and rode away into the fields with her ferret, Cosmos.

Chapter Seven ☼

Shadow Bone Queen

Ivan got on his horse, chased Jasmine, and when he almost caught up with her, he yelled, "Jasmine! Jasmine! Stop! Talk with me."

Jasmine looked back and saw Ivan right behind her, so she pulled on the reins for Breezy to stop and then got off. Neither said a word for a while. They walked in silence, and then Ivan said, "Jasmine, I didn't mean to hurt your feelings. I just didn't want to engage into something that might lead us into things that might prevent us from accomplishing our goal; you know, finding the golden eggs."

"Ivan, you need to tell me these things, rather than turning away. I'm not a mind reader."

"I'm sorry, Jasmine. I shall be more careful of my actions."

They walked for a while and then got back on their horses and headed back to camp.

By the time, they got back, right away, they could see something had happened because everyone was silent; dancing had stopped, and the food was placed back in the boxes.

"What's wrong?" Jasmine asked as she moved over to her grandmother.

Then Bevin appeared, and said, "the neighboring town from here has been attacked, and we should go there at the earliest sun appearance. We need to bed ourselves in and be ready for the early morning hour."

"Yes, Grandmother, but you should stay here and allow your wounds to heal."

"No Granddaughter, I must go. I've re-wrapped my wounds, and I'll be fine."

When Jasmine woke, she discovered that she was lying on the soft feathers, and her bedding had been tossed a few feet away. She moved over, picked up the bedding, and saw her three ferrets hugging one another and fast asleep. She chuckled, and quickly put them back into her pouch and stretched. Sunlight glittered, and the air was full of a crisp chilliness. She remembered, they had to ride out to the neighboring town and quickly ran to the water and started bathing her face, arms and legs.

After the wagons and horses were loaded up, the men washed and clothed, and had eaten a light meal, then got on their horses and bellowed out. "Off to the town, we shall go!"

Jasmine rode beside the wagon with Ivan on the other side looking at her, and when she looked back, he winked. Her face flushed and she smiled at him. Her grandmother watched the two and was pleased. She smiled to herself and wrapped the bear blanket tightly around her.

The plan was to send in Ivan and Jasmine to investigate the town before the others followed. As Jasmine got off Breezy, she moved over near Ivan, and as they walked into the town, thousands of dead blackbirds fell upon them, but they didn't see anyone.

Jasmine whistled, and the others began riding in fast and hard and Breezy ran up and stood in front of her. She patted his head and gave him his apple and climbed on his back. Ramara got off the wagon and led her white Arabian over to Jasmine and said, "Consa is arriving soon. I shall wait here while you and Ivan search the town."

More dead birds fell, and they all ran for cover into the empty buildings. The armies walked in the middle of the square, trying to figure out what was going on.

Ramara turned to see Consa walking toward her, and when she stood next to her, she whispered, "I've got a bad feeling about this place. It's quite eerie."

Consa took her crystal stone out of her pouch, held it up and said, "This is an evil place. It is the grounds of the Shadow Bone Queen. She is insane and will drive anyone who enters, mad."

"Shadow Bone Queen? I thought this town was attacked." Ramara said.

"Yes, it was. I feared the Vikon's were taking over the town, and I didn't want that to happen, so I called all the armies at hand, but it seems the town is dead."

"We can't have the Vikons take over another town or village. They must be stopped." Ramara said.

"Yes, stopped forever! They've taken over far too many villages."

"We will form armies together and stop them!" moaned Ramara.

"We will, but in this town, the queen rises out of hell and torments the people. They say the Shadow Bone Queen is cursed by the Gods and that is why there is such destruction in this town. No human can live among such an evil queen. It is told that the queen can stay only within the boundaries of this town." Consa said as she turned to look at more birds dropping.

"If this is so, then we must find out how this is done?"

Consa smiled and said, "Yes, we must."

"I wonder where she is hiding."

"She cannot leave freely because she is bound to this place for eternity. Look over there Ramara, the shadows!"

"Shadows?"

"Yes, the shadows are the shadow people who long ago died. We need to leave now Ramara, the Vikons are not here."

"But Consa, how are we to learn how it is they have found her in this small town."

"Yes, we must, but all those black shadows are going from place to place, and the men are becoming uneasy and starting to get confused."

"Consa, are they the ones that make men hear voices in their heads and unable to figure out the words?" Ramara asked.

"Yes, they are ghosts still hanging around their own town. They are servants to the queen."

"Servants to the queen? Is it not her who killed them in the first place?"

"It is so, but they are as crazy as her, now."

Jasmine got off Breezy and stood with her magical sword drawn, then holding it up with both hands she said, "Show yourself, Shadow Bone Queen." Within minutes a big wind came up and the dust swirled around, and the chilling Shadow Bone Queen appeared. Her skin was gray and shiny as the full moon. Her robe was like the blackness of the darkest night. She pointed towards five of the soldiers and they immediately turned into skeletons. "It is I, Jasmine from Valley of the Yellow Stones. Why do you stand there calling my name?"

"I want to leave this evil place and your dark force stands in my way. Release me."

"Why would you think I'd let you leave? May I remind you, you're in my kingdom and I'm the queen of it."

"You have blood on your hands that will never wash off. You are bound here within this small town and I, for one will find out how to keep you in hell away from this town."

The Queen lifted her hands to the sky and a big black swarm of locusts appeared over the armies men. Jasmine rubbed her magic ring and lifted it to the heavens and disappeared.

"Run it's the black plague, run for your lives." the army men screamed. The men ran into darkened buildings while others stood with their shields held high, but it did not protect them.

Consa and Ramara walked over to Jasmine after she reappeared and stood next to her while they watched her stretch out her arms toward the queen and a lightning bolt came forward directed toward the queen, but she put her hand up and stopped it. She cackled with an eerie noise and said, “Is that all you’ve got to attack with, Jasmine? You know nothing of being a queen.”

Ramara and Consa held their arms out toward the queen and before they could send out large bolts of lightning directed at the queen, a Light Elf stepped out toward the Shadow Bone Queen and lifted her staff and a great light came upon the queen and encircled her while it swirled around and around, going faster and faster until the queen disintegrated into thin air. Within minutes, the sunlight shined upon the dark city and you could hear the shadow people crying out as they were being burned into ashes that fell to the fields purifying the soil.

Consa looked at the Light Elf and said, “Thank you. Where did you come from? I have not seen you before this day.”

The Light Elf chuckled and said, “I was in the Forest and saw you walking toward the queen’s evil town and knew you were falling into a trap. I am Melody. My people put her here long ago because she is an evil, insane queen.” Melody’s white hair waved down her back like fresh fallen snow. She stood with her sparkling large black eyes and smiled at Consa as she moved over near Ramara and Jasmine. Her pale skin had not a blemish on it and her beauty stood out and impressed Jasmine. She noticed Melody carried a magic bow with a glowing flame from an arrow.

Melody said, “I hear you are searching for the Sacred Golden Eggs. I am the purest of the Elf’s. I am the powerful one that lives in the forest, going from one village to another, setting things right. I am at your service. I will help you find your golden eggs.”

Jasmine stepped closer to Melody and smiled. “You speak with a pure tongue and I shall be honored to have you in my army to find the golden eggs.”

“Very well, when the time comes, you take this feather and hold it up to the sky and I shall come to you.”

Jasmine took the feather Melody offered and stuck it behind her ear and then placed her hair down over it, knowing she'd get a string to attach the feather and place it around her neck.

Melody said, "There is danger all around you here. You must be more careful about calling out to people you know nothing about. The queen could have had you with only your bones lying on the ground."

Chapter Eight ☼

Ruddey and Hickey

Consa, the gatekeeper, left to return back to her kingdom, the Secret Garden of the Ancients, after thanking Ramara and Jasmine for coming so promptly. "I shall go prepare for capturing all the Vikons and will meet you with all your armies on the Vikon Mountain at the third sunrise."

Ivan announced that two hundred warriors would stay in Shadow Bone Queen's town; rename it and set it up as an army base for all those in war against the Vikons. We shall elect a captain this very night and build the town into a town of light instead of a dark one. We will bring all our equipment here as a home base."

Ramara reached out her hand to Ivan and said, "I suggest your two hundred warriors begin immediately to rebuild this town, while you and Jasmine go into the forest and locate the men who ran away."

Ivan agreed. "Yes, you speak wisdom Ramara." he turned around and gave his orders to the men standing at attention.

Ramara went to Jasmine and told her she would ride with the men returning back to the campsite and would meet her and Ivan on the Vikon Mountain on the third sunrise.

Jasmine and Ivan got on their horses and began riding toward the forest. After riding for a long time, they heard a voice saying, "Help me! Oh, I can't get out. I am surely going to die. Oh, woe is me! Please, somebody, help me!"

As they moved toward the crying, they saw a large pit and again heard the pleading voice, "can't you just shut up? I am sick and tired of hearing you complain when you know we're going to rot in this pit."

The dragon moaned and said, "But I don't want to rot in this pit."

"No one will ever hear us down here, thanks to you… you… crazy old Dragon."

"Ohhh…I am so thirsty!"

"Please, shut up! You're going to drive me insane!"

Jasmine and Ivan got off their horses, looked down into the large pit, and smiled after they saw a cute little dragon.

"Ohhhhh, look! Someone is here to save us!" cried the dragon.

The little voice said, "Oh, you are just imagining things again like you did yesterday when you said someone was coming and it was only a bird that flew by."

"Hello," said Jasmine as she looked down in the pit.

The little voice said, "Oh, look someone is really up there,"

"Oh, please won't you get us out of this pit. We have been here for days and we're powerfully hungry. We can't escape this dreadful place because my neck is chained, and I can't move. I will give you anything you ask if you will please get us out of here."

Ivan asked, "Who is with you?"

The little voice said, "Look closer down here under the dreadful dragon and then you will see me."

Jasmine and Ivan looked closely and saw a little fairy.

"You are so tiny to be with such a big dragon," Jasmine said as she chuckled at the difference in their sizes.

"I know this is true, but we were put here by the angry

Pilons. They left us here to die."

"Ohhh, please help us." The dragon said.

"Oh dragon…you big…oh you… it's so like you interrupting me. You big over stuff bag of fire! Can you believe I have been stuck here all this time with this jabbering dragon, all he does is talk, talk, talk?"

Jasmine looked at Ivan, and they laughed so hard that they couldn't respond for a moment. Once they got control of themselves, they looked at the poor sad dragon and said, "Hold on I'll get my rope and get you both out."

"Won't you please get us a drink of water; my palate is so dry I have no fire left?"

Jasmine grabbed the water bag from her saddle, and the dragon opened his large mouth, and Jasmine poured water into it, and a small drop fell onto the fairy and she coughed as if she were drowning. Ivan came back with the rope and dropped it down beside them and then climbed down into the pit with his sword and hit the chain until it broke and then told the dragon to climb up out of the pit. It was a struggle, but the three of them made it up.

Right away Jasmine noticed the little fairy had an injured wing and the dragon was weak, but after Jasmine gave them her cheese and meat, they felt better.

"Yes, indeed he really made a mess of it this time. King Pilon we put into the pit of death to die, you see, because Ruddey caught a cold and started coughing. Well, he coughed fire all over the king and queen leaving them standing with no hair or clothes. They had soot all over their faces and were totally embarrassed. They screamed as they ran naked into the palace. His people laughed so hard it was heard throughout the whole kingdom."

"Oh my, I bet the King was displeased, "said Jasmine as she chuckled.

"Yes, he was, and it took him a couple of days before he'd come out of the castle," giggled the fairy. "Oh, I'm Hickey, the

Fairy of Minalia, the keeper of all the dragons of Pilon, or I was. The king was so angry that he threw me into the pit along with Ruddey here."

"The King was mighty angry at me, but I told the king I was sick, but he didn't care. He only cared about his people laughing at him." Ruddey said.

"Oh you…you…bag of fire…you're a real klutz." Hickey said as she lifted her wing and noticed it was already getting better.

Ivan suggested they go up the hill around the tall dry trees and they would come to a town called the Shadow Bone Queen's town. As soon as he mentioned the queen the fairy screamed, "oh no, we can't go there!"

Jasmine said, "Shadow Bone Queen is no longer, and we've made her town into a safe place. It's where the army is, and they will take care of you both. We would go with you, but we have to find some men that fled before we go."

"Just tell them Sir Ivan and Jasmine sent you there to be looked after," Ivan said as he climbed on his horse.

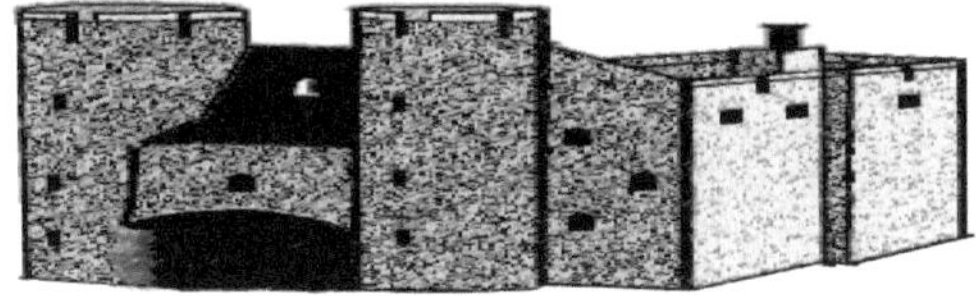

Chapter Nine ☼

War on the Vikon Mountain

Ivan and Jasmine rounded up all the different armies, from different towns and villages that had joined them, led them back to the Shadow Bone Queen's town, and as they entered in through the tall wooden gates the armies men had built, Ivan could see the new town's name had been established; Town of Light.

Jasmine raced up beside Ivan and said, "It is now the Town of Light, and within these gates will be discussions on how to rid all kingdoms of the Vikon terror. They kill for the sake of killing. They storm villages and shed blood wherever they go. The Town of Light will end the Vikon's evil ways, and when it does, then it will be renamed, *The Healing Town*. We then won't use it for the army equipment and place of stay. We'll use it for all the people who were damaged during this war, and they shall live here to heal."

"I like that idea and the name," Ivan said as he smiled at Jasmine.

Right away, Jasmine, saw the cute little dragon, Ruddey, and Hickey, the Fairy of Minalia. They were lying under a tree resting with one of the army's men tending to them.

"Hello, Jasmine!" Hickey hollered.

Jasmine walked over to Hickey, the fairy and said, "I see you're looking better than when I last saw you."

"Oh yes, Jasmine, I am as good as new. I'm glad I saw you again because I wanted to tell you that if ever you need me to help you find the sacred golden eggs, I will."

"Thank you, Hickey, I might take you up on that."

"I'm so tiny that I can fly and grab an egg when necessary."

Ruddey interrupted and said, "I can shoot fire out my

mouth too."

"Oh, you clumsy dragon, you'd probably burn yourself up and me too," Hickey said as she laughed.

Cosmos, the ferret, jumped out of Jasmines pouch and ran over to Ruddey, grabbed the hat off his head that the soldier had given him, and then ran off, leaving all three laughing.

Ivan summoned, Jasmine to the armies meeting discussing the Vikon Mountain. She excused herself, hurried over quickly, and sat down at the front table.

"Men, men, listen up. We have business to attend to, and tomorrow at first sun up, we began our journey to the Vikon Mountain. We need to carefully plan our attack. Does anyone have any suggestions? Speak now, if you do, because once we get to the battle field there will no questions to be asked," Ivan spoke loudly for all to hear.

The Captain of the West army stood up and said, "I reckon we should start our front-line men to the first-attack, then wait a few minutes, and then our second-line men could go forward."

Ivan nodded and then said, "Good plan, Captain. I think we cross half the distance before nightfall. Then the next day, we arrive as planned at first sunrise." He then paused.

Gambol, a large figure of man who was the captain's best man stood up looking annoyed with stopping at half-point and said, "Don't be a fool, Sir Ivan, we need to go all the way, then sleep and prepare for our attack at sunrise."

"We will go half way as I stated, Gambol, but you made a good suggestion. You will go ahead, taking a few men with you to check out the surroundings and then wait on the west side of the mountain for us."

Jasmine stood up and said, "I think that is a good plan Ivan. I will move to the east mountain with Ramara, taking 100 men."

To Ivan's dismay, he realized that he would not be with Jasmine as the battle began. He frowned and then said, "I will go with you, and Ramara, Jasmine, and the Captain of the west will take the men to meet up with Gambol and his men."

Before the meeting had ended Ramara lifted her hands and said, "Not one and I mean not one leave a Vikon behind alive. If you have to follow the bastard, follow him, but make sure he falls dead to the ground!"

The rest of the men cheered, and they ended the meeting with their cups full of wine, and tables filled with food that Bevin had sent over.

The next morning, the journey began with all men lined up, the drummer hit the first beat, and they all galloped out of the Town of Light. Ruddey and Hickey were riding in the wagon while Jasmine and Ivan, led the army out the gates toward Vikon Mountain.

By the time they had reached half way point, they were ready for rest and food. They discussed the attack until it was time to get some sleep and by the next morning, everybody was geared up to attack. Ramara kept rising her arms to the sky saying, "Not one Vikon standing."

The last stage of the journey to Vikon Mountain came, and the energies were flying with the men reared up to fight. Away to the northeast there was a shimmer of lightening under the black skies. Most horrible of all, the air was full of fumes; breathing wasn't easy, and Ivan wondered what was going on.

The mountains crawled up ever nearer and the men were filled with rage to fight, to kill the Vikons; the ones who continued to rape the villager's woman and burn their entire villages down to ashes. There was no reasoning with them. They were out to take all the land and the people in it.

Gambol sent out a messenger to tell Ivan and the others that Consa had arrived early and had burned the gates leading into Vikon cities. She and her men were fighting Vikons, and Jasmine knew they soon would be too.

Drums rolled and fires hurdled up. All the doors of the Vikons swung back wide. Out of them came hundreds of

Vikons on horses coming as swift as roaring water beating against rocks, coming fast and hard. Horse huffs sounded on the soil like thunder as Ivan looked up, he imagined the mountain eastside bubbling with men's blood. He waved and ordered the battle. His men raced toward the Vikons.

The wind was blowing, and arrows shot out like a wave of lightening in the sky. As the drums sounded, men attacked, and screaming was heard for miles. An arrow raced past, and he threw up his sword and screamed to the heavens to forgive this day. The sun was now climbing toward the mountain tops and the threatening haze gleamed of war.

The Vikons came with their cold cries, words of death, and then all hope of living was quenched. Men were falling off their horses while arrows shot out across the mountain top. Jasmine stayed on the eastside of the mountain, watching as she eyed, Ivan riding hard and striking out with his bloody sword dripping. The crying continued to be heard for miles and miles. When Jasmine saw Ivan fall to the ground, her heart raced like a mighty wind blowing over the heavens. She jerked off the feather from her string that the Elf, Melody, had given her and lifted it to the heavens, summoning her. She looked again, and saw Ivan revive himself painfully from the ground. For a moment, he was dazed and shook his head forgetting where he was and then all of a sudden, he remembered all the wretchedness and anguish, jumped back upon his horse and raced to the top of the mountain.

Chapter Ten ☼
Jasmine and Melody

With a gasp, Jasmine raced her horse toward Ivan to make sure he was alright. As she neared, he cast himself on the ground and checked his side where he had been hit. Jasmine jumped off Breezy and ran to him. It was anguish greater than Ivan had ever thought that he could bear. He was in pain, and so much that he could no longer swallow even a mouthful of water. Smoke from the mountain made it look as though a dense fog was covering it. Lightening shimmer over the mountain and the skies were black and drops of rain began to come down from the heavens. An awful pain waved over Ivan until he thought he was going into blackness. Jasmine lowered her body beside him and tore a piece of her clothing, dampened it and began to wipe away the blood from his side. She saw that it was a deep wound and she knew she needed to get him to safety. She turned to see why Breezy was kicking the ground and saw Melody, the Elf standing straight up and singing.

I stand upon Mother Earth
The universe is Divine
It sends me Light
So, I can do my angel work
For I am sent as a guide
Helping those in need
The universe is Divine
When we are kind
The world rings out melodies
The Universe is Divine
It's hard for us to contemplate
A world that is ageless in time

For we are all of God's chosen
With blessing so sublime

After Melody finished her song, she went to Ivan and laid her hand on Ivan's wound and chanted until the wound disappeared. Ivan thanked her profusely as he got up and climbed back on his horse. Jasmine jumped on Breezy, and they went toward the battle once again.

Ivan felt so inspirited that if all the Vikons in the world had attacked him he wouldn't have retreated one-inch. A Vikon seeing him in such a state began to shower stones on him. Ivan caught them and threw them back. "I throw these stones at you, you despicable warrior who kills for the sake of killing. I pay no heed, come closer and stone me, come, draw near, beset me as best you can, for you will soon see how you are made to pay for your madness and your boldness."

The Vikon threw his last stone and Ivan swung back his sword and knocked him to the ground as he passed him by. Ivan seized him by his arm and tied him back to a big oak tree and flogged him half to death and left him to die. "It will be a day in hell before you flee me and act upon killing for the sake of killing. Raping women and killing children. Bid your time and die!"

Jasmine and the armies continued their battle, while Ivan rode off over the hill chasing another Vikon. Death was spread over the mountains while some men were lying in their agony and horses trampled over them, crushing whatever they stepped on while the horsemen screamed, "You won't live when this day is through!"

Jasmine got off her horse carrying her pouch as she neared the Vikon town. She dropped her leather shield, raised her lance with both hands, and dealt the approaching Vikon so powerful a blow to the head that he fell to the ground in such a sad state that had it been followed by another blow he wouldn't have known what hit him.

Jasmine replaced her armor and continued pacing back and

forth with eagerness to retrieve the eggs. After a while another Vikon, not knowing what had happened because the first one still lay stunned, also came toward her and she let him have the same. She looked at the temple and ran as fast as she could until she got inside and right away, she saw one of her boxes that they had stolen. She moved swiftly over to it and lifted the lid and saw one sacred golden egg. She picked it up and before she could put it in her pouch, a Vikon attacked her, sending her a blow that knocked her to the ground. Cosmos grabbed the golden egg and ran while the Vikon was hitting her again and again.

Ivan stormed in and saw what the Vikon was doing to Jasmine and drew back his sword and ended his life immediately. He picked up Jasmine and quickly took her back to his horse and whistled for Breezy. She came and stood before him and he threw Jasmine over the saddle and they rode out of the town to the other side of the mountain.

Ivan dropped Jasmine off near the stream with Melody so he could go back and help with the army. He gently laid her on a blanket and Melody told him to go and she would look after Jasmine. Shortly after Ivan left three Vikons came and threw a sack over Melody's head and tied it tightly around her neck while the other one grabbed Jasmine.

They threw them on their horses and quickly went to the Vikon camp and left them with the guards. Jasmines hands were tied so she couldn't rub her ring. She became frantic but told herself to calm her spirits or she wouldn't be ready for any new trouble coming her way.

The guards threw Jasmine and Melody to the ground as they entered their prison cell and laughed. Melody quickly began to untie Jasmine and then asked. "Are you okay?"

"Yes, I'm alright. How are you?"

Trying to compose themselves while sitting there on the cold, damp dark floor, they didn't lose a moment and began to discuss how they could escape this God-awful dark place. The other prisoners overheard Jasmine and Melody whispering and knew their fate; it was going to be death.

One prisoner spoke up and said, “You speak of escape?”

Jasmine said, “Yes, there is only one path in order to fulfill this dark place; we must kill them all.”

“Some of us will have to sacrifice ourselves to save others. Are you willing?” Melody asked.

“What is it you want us to do?”

“Let us think for a moment, and then we’ll tell you. “ Jasmine said. “Before we do anything, we need to send Jazzell with a note back to camp so the men will be on stand-by.”

Jasmine reached into her pocket and grabbed the stone her grandmother had given her, wrapped it in a piece of her clothing and attached it on the inside of Jazzell’s collar. “Run Jazzell, run like the wind back to grandmother.”

Jazzell squeezed in between the bars and ran as fast as she could, out of the cell and over toward the mountain where Ramara was camping.

Jasmine turned to Melody and said, “She will know what to do. We must wait. If need be, I will rub my ring and disappear, but know I shall be back for you.”

Shortly after the sun rose up over the mountain the next morning, the guards came in and took Melody and Jasmine to Arbaddon where the guards threw them to the ground in front of him and said kneel to our leader. They both kneeled before a dark wooly giant of a man.

“Who are you and what are you doing in my village?”

“I’m Jasmine, and this is my friend, Melody.”

The big leader took his hand under Jasmine's chin and said, “Look at me when I am speaking to you!” He then turned to his guards and said, “Take them away guards; we shall have entertainment with them in the arena, begging for their lives, on this very day. Make sure the lions you put in the arena are hungry.”

Meanwhile, Cosmos was scurrying around, trying not to be

seen carrying the egg he had taken from the Vikons. At the perfect moment he was going to race back to camp. He saw that perfect moment and ran as fast as he could until reaching the campsite. Ramara saw him running toward her, but she didn't see Jasmine.

"Oh, something is wrong. I feel it in my tired bones," said Ramara.

"Men! Men! Quickly go get Ivan. I need him immediately. Tell him something has happened to Jasmine. Hurry. Don't linger one moment longer! Go! Now Cosmos, hand me that golden egg."

Soon after, Jazzell raced to Ramara and began making a baby crying sound. She twisted and turned and pawed Ramara until she said, "What is it Jazzell?" Ramara picked her up and saw the stone with a piece of Jasmine's clothing attached to her collar. She tore it off Jazzell's collar and screamed, "Oh, no! Oh, no! The Vikons have captured Ramara and Melody. Ramara went to the campfire and bellowed out to the fire, "Fire, show us, Jasmine."

Up came a cloud of smoke in the fire and they could see a hologram and Jasmine's head come up from the flames and said, "*grandmother Melody and I are in prison, but now they've put us near the arena where the lions will soon come and feast upon us! Get a plan together and help us escape, please…now!*"

"Yes granddaughter, we will."

Before Ramara could say anymore, Jasmine disappeared and the flames died out.

As soon as Ivan received the news, he saw red. His heart began beating faster than two drums in a ceremony. He calmed himself enough to sit down with the leaders to devise a plan.

"I've got it! I will take some of you men, and we'll sneak into camp dressed like Vikons." Ivan said as he rubbed his hand over his face still thinking. "We need to find their uniforms. Pico, you will go with me to get those uniforms. I think I know where they store them."

All dressed in Vikon clothing they neared the guards and immediately began to tie them up. They shoved them into the empty wagon and placed a blanket over them; out of sight. All the men and Ivan spread out and got passed the entrance and were shocked at what they saw.

King Arbaddon and his wife, Lilith were getting ready for the most talked about entertainment of the year and were excited by their lust for the blood promised tonight in the arena. Both loved to watch the suffering and tortures, but tonight it was going to be especially exciting with Jasmine as the main attraction. But the first ones appearing in the arena was the older prisoners who would be made to kill each other or be stoned to death. Then the second showing would be the giant and five men and lastly the two women that the king promised would be well worth the wait.

King Arbaddon loved to hear the screams of women dying, and he could hardly wait to see the terror on Jasmine's face. Arbaddon was a mentally ill man who sent his men out to attack villagers for no known reason other than the thrill of it. *Oh, if only her grandmother could see her now*, he thought. The Vikons were being seated in the bleachers and shortly after the men lay dead, they sent in the giant and then chained him in the middle of the arena where he was to fight five men at a time while they were chained to each other. Each man had a sword and a shield. Arbaddon laughed each time one of the five fell face down in the dirt as the giant chased and attacked them on the arms and legs with his sword. The crowds roared with excitement and laughed at their flow of blood. The five fell to their death within minutes and the crowd screamed with excitement.

Then the loud cheering of the crowd alerted Ivan to who had entered the arena; Jasmine and Melody who looked frightened and tried to run, but they were pushed back into the arena. Jasmine landed face down with Melody beside her.

Ivan wanted to run and help them, but he knew he would be killed, and his attempt would be in vain. Jasmine knew all she had to do was rub the ring, but she wouldn't do that until it was absolutely necessary because she didn't wish to leave Melody.

All of a sudden Melody stood up and looked up toward the sky and began singing. Her voice was so beautiful that everyone in the kingdom stopped laughing and was so mesmerized by her that they stared in amazement. They had never heard beautiful melodies that came out of her mouth.

"She has the voice of an angel." a voice whispered in the crowd.

The lions began to lie down on the ground licking their paws. Jasmine stood up and asked the universe to give them the power to overcome this ruthless madness.

Melody stopped singing, and Jasmine said to King Arbaddon, "I am the daughter of Cyrus, from the Valley of the Yellow Stones. You have killed and taken our sacred eggs, and you will die on this glorious day."

King Arbaddon looked at Jasmine and laughed as he pointed at her and said, "My people, this peasant girl thinks death is upon me this day when it is, she who will die!"

Lilith nudged Arbaddon and said, "Look, my husband, the lions are lying down."

"How can that be? Get up you foolish lions. Get up, I say." King Arbaddon screamed.

The wind began to blow fast and hard and as it got stronger the ground began shaking; like an earthquake, they had never seen. The volcano at the top of the mountain started to blow fire, and the people started to run. Building started to tumble, and Jasmine lifted her hand with the magic stone in it and pointed it at Arbaddon and a wind came from it and blew him across his throne. Lilith began screaming as fire came toward her and within seconds burned her in ashes.

Chapter Eleven ☼

Crystal City

King Arbaddon rose and his black cloud came over the arena, and Jasmine took her stones, and dirt with the prisoner's blood, and threw it into the air and King Arbaddon's black sky turned into a white shaft of light that glittered and sent out sparkles all over the crowd.

"You've lost your powers, King Arbaddon," Jasmine bellowed out.

Arbaddon commanded his soldiers to kill Jasmine and Melody. Ivan and his men drew their swords and started to kill the Vikons. The horn blew and the leaders of the army surrounded the town and began to fight while screaming, "Kill them all!"

The army sent out a blast of fire and large stones, hitting and killing the Vikons. Vikons fell dead everywhere and all the while the ground was still shaking and moving beneath their feet.

King Arbaddon started to run fast and hard to get away from the terror. He didn't get far because a lion that had escaped, grabbed his robe and began to tear him apart as he screamed in agony with terror, but was called off. He lay wounded, but alive. In an angry voice he shouted," If it's the last thing I do, I will kill Jasmine!"

Ivan threw Jasmine her sword and she began to fight. She lifted it up high in the sky and thundering began sounding and Vikons turned to ashes.

"Release the prisoners so they can fight with us." Jasmine yelled to Melody, "Go, Melody. We need help!"

Melody ran like a rapid storm into the arena where the prisoners were being held and quickly freed them. She handed them weapons and soon after, they killed the guards, and then hurried to help Ivan.

"Did you hear what King Arbaddon threatened to do?" Jasmine said with dirt all over her face.

"Yes, I did, we need to end his warring ways! Go back to Ramara and see about going to Crystal Temple." moaned Ivan.

Jasmine looked over the bloody land, turned and let out a whistle and Breezy stood before her. She jumped on his back and raced to Ramara. She noticed right away that Ramara was pacing as if she wanted to do something, but what, she didn't know. Her face was drawn, and Jasmine could see she was agitated and the added worry about her granddaughter had really gotten her down. She looked up and saw Jasmine and moved over to her with her arms open wide.

"Oh, granddaughter! Oh, Granddaughter, you are safe. I worried so!"

Jasmine flew into her arms and they both stood and cried. "Grandmother, I think we should go to Crystal City. Melody will go with us and Consa will appear soon. So, pack up your things and let's go. We must hurry."

Jasmine, Ramara, and Melody were on their way when Consa appeared and then the four rode into the Crystal City together. They had heard many stories of such a place but had never been there and on the east side of the city stood a pyramid temple which was made entirely of crystal stones. It sparkled and shimmered like no city they had ever seen. Their hearts beat against their chest as they looked at it and broke out in tears of joy. The four of them got off their horses and walked up the high steps to reach the top of the temple's entrance. As they approached, they saw two large wooden doors with the *Tree of Life* attached to the entire door. They stood in awe at the magnificent door with its golden branches made of gold and brilliant color of green leaves.

"Ah, this has such grand carvings and stands so eloquent." Ramara said as he gazed at it and then pushed on the door as she turned its gold handle. The four walked in and at once noticed a slight breeze blowing through the large billowy white silk curtains.

Jasmine cried out, “Ahh, they must hang thirty feet high.”

The sunlight made the crystals shimmer with rainbow colored prisms and sent it through-out the beautiful temple. They looked at one another with fascination as they felt energy and power like they had ever felt before. Suddenly a couple Crystal Priests, wearing white robes walked out from the side entrance while two others stood on each side of the door holding flaming torches.

“Please…come closer. We have been expecting you. Welcome!” The priest said as he smiled and right away noticed he glowed as if a light was around his face. “We know of the sacred golden eggs. You must get them back from King Arbaddon, and I’m here to tell you that the Universe will award you strong powers to do just that. You will conquer this wicked leader.” Tuari, the priest, said. “Come closer. I’ll take you to the altar.”

As they stood before the altar, a gentle wind moved over their bodies and they felt an overwhelming amount of energy. Shortly after, Tuari poured them wine, which he called his special wine with an herb mixture poured into it. He handed Ramara the gold shiny cup and told her to sip and then pass it on to the others. The Crystal Priest prayed to the Universe. “Give these brave souls the light source for great wisdom and power to do battle with the wicked one Arbaddon.”

Ramara stepped forward and handed the priest the golden egg Cosmos had brought to her and said, “Crystal Priest, please keep this one sacred golden egg in a safe place until this war is over.”

He took it and placed it on the altar and all of a sudden, a white light came down upon them and moved through-out the Crystal Temple and filled it with brilliant light filled with prisms and bright colors. The colors swirled around and around as the wind blew it sending out a rose fragrance. The curtains blew higher and the fire torches were flickering in the wind. A priest started smudging the altar with sage as a white light was coming from the ceiling and touching the top of their heads and moved on down caressing their entire bodies. The four stood like tall statues as more and more light moved down over them. After a long while, the light gradually disappeared, and the wind died down as did the prisms. The curtains were still, but the fragrance remained.

"You four have the power and wisdom to defeat this evil man. Know that the Universe is with you, always. Now, take one of these stones; Crystals, Citrine and Aamethyst. They will serve you well. Just place them in your pouch and believe. The stones will always protect you." Tuari, the high priest said as he handed them the stones. "These stones will remove any negative energy and set you in the positive light of your mind. They will guide you. Fear not!"

As they got to the large door to leave, Tuari said, "The time is at hand and the divine order in the Universe has lifted your heart to liberate you from all fear through the true spiritual justice that exists in all things. You are free to create a future for this kingdom. May the great white spirit follow you wherever you may go."

They left and as they hurried to their horses, they felt the power that all things were possible for them to end this war, get their sacred golden eggs and powerfully felt all things were possible. They saw through clearer eyes and knew they had been changed forever. Their minds were settled on what action they should take.

On the road ahead leading back to camp, they sang songs of power and soon as they rode up to the campsite, they got off their horses and called a meeting.

All the village leaders, armies and the four women sat down in a five-tear circle and discussed their plans.

"We will fight the last battle, winning of course and return our sacred golden eggs to their rightful place so our weather conditions improve, and we build new and better villages for all the land." Jasmine said with wisdom about her.

Everyone began to cheer in excitement as their energies reached levels of great height.

"Listen, men, King Arbaddon has to be stopped, the leader of the Vikons, so early morning we will break camp and move toward the battle field once again; to end this bloody war. This will be our last battle with the Vikons." Ramara stated as she placed her hand up in the air and shouted, "Gone with the Vikons!"

Temple

Chapter Twelve ☼

Jasmine Retrieves another Golden Egg

"Kill the Vikons!" The army's men shouted.

Early the next morning, the men loaded up their weapons, soon after eating and loading up the wagon, Cosmos ran over and snatched up an apple out of the box and threw it over in front of Breezy. She looked at it and then up at Jasmine. She stood up and walked over to the apple, bent down and picked it up and placed it in Breezy's mouth while all the men chuckled.

Within the hour, they headed out on their journey feeling powerful and ready for battle. Along the path, Ivan caught up with them stating he had the battlefield ready for them and they'd stop in short of it and discuss their immediate plan.

Jasmine smiled over at Ivan, and he smiled at her as he rode on up ahead of the army.

Jasmine got off Breezy as Ivan did Gallo and they walked over near the stream while they discussed the day's adventures. She told him about the Crystal Temple as his eyes lighted up and smiled. He knew Jasmine looked calmer, yet full of energy too.

After they returned, Ivan discussed their entry plan onto the battlefield, and then they all got on their horses and rode within a mile of the Vikon battlefields and noticed right away many Vikon men were still laying on the ground in their own blood. Not many had been buried.

"Okay Granddaughter, our first task is to get the golden eggs. The ferrets will grab them and run back to the campsite, from there Melody will take them."

"Yes, Grandmother, and also Hickey, the fairy offered to fly over and get an egg too. This will happen while the men finish off the rest of the Vikons."

Melody moved over to Jasmine and her grandmother and whispered, "Look at that tall mountain with all the fires, there's thousands of Vikons, but as the Crystal Priest stated, we will win this battle."

"Have no fear men, we will win this battle with the help of the Universe. Let's defeat these Vikons and get our freedom back." Jasmine hollered.

As the hour hit midnight, Ramara and Jasmine and the three ferrets tucked in her pouch moved down toward the Vikon Temple, passing the guards with caution and entering into the temple where the golden eggs were. Right away, Jasmine sent Cosmos and Philo in while Jazzell stayed behind just in case anything went wrong. Melody waited so the ferrets could bring the eggs to her for safe keeping.

Cosmos and Philo started searching for the eggs; sniffing for the scent of the eggs. During their search, Cosmos knocked over a cup and a Vikon guard saw him. Cosmos scurried into some boxes trying to get away from him, but the guard cornered Cosmos and was just about to smash him when Philo bit him on the leg and then ran. The Vikon fell back into the nearby cabinet, and it went tumbling down as he cursed. "You beast of an animal; I'll get you! Those damn pesky rodents!"

The Vikon men wondering what the commotion was about hurried over to see what was going on while Cosmos and Philo got to the building where the eggs were and hid behind its box until things calmed down.

Melody ran over toward Jasmine and said, "I've taken Ramara's place, and she's back at the campsite. She's feeling a bit tired."

"Good enough, let's see where the ferrets are and then head back."

As they searched in a small storage room, Jasmine heard a light noise and moved over near a box, shoving it aside Jasmine gasped; there sat the Sacred Golden Eggs box and behind it were her two ferrets. She smiled and slipped her hand into the box and lifted out one of the golden eggs. All of a sudden, she heard someone coming. She grabbed up her ferrets and rubbed her magic ring and disappeared. She had visualized the campsite where Ramara was and instantly appeared beside her grandmother napping. She stood up and shook her body when she began feeling dizzy.

"Granddaughter! You're back. Oh, you got one of the golden eggs."

"Yes, Grandmother, I did, but I must go back and get Melody. She is still searching for the golden egg box. I will take Cosmos back with me."

"Jasmine, when you return, and this war is over, I need to talk to you about going to Consa's Secret Garden. I think I need a good rest and go into withdrawal. You are now ready to take my place as the shaman, so I felt quite comfortable leaving."

"Grandmother, are you ill?"

"No Jasmine, I'm not ill. I'm tired. I'm old and need to withdraw and spend the rest of my days in Consa's garden. You know we've discussed that a day would come for me to do just that."

"I know Grandmother. I know we have, but I'm not ready for you to leave me yet."

"Go, Granddaughter. Go! We shall discuss this when you return. Melody is waiting. Go!"

"Yes, Grandmother, I'm going, and we will discuss this when I return."

Jasmine rubbed her ring and visualized the storage room, and again, she instantly appeared back where the box sat. The box had been closed, and it appeared a chain had been placed around it. She quietly moved out of the room looking for Melody and ran smack into her as she turned to go down the hallway. "Oh Jasmine, I've been searching for you everywhere."

"I went back to camp, but I've returned with Cosmos. We must go get those eggs."

"Yes, I know where they are Jasmine. I saw a guard put a chain around the box and mumble to himself that one of them had been taken. He accused a guard of taking it, and they fought over it. I think he killed him. I slipped back into another room and decided to come out again when you ran into me."

Just as they decided to go in search of something to cut the chain Cosmos appeared in the doorway with an egg. "How in the world did Cosmos get into the box?" Jasmine asked.

"I don't know, but let's go see."

"No, Melody, wait here. I am going to go back to Ramara and take her this egg. This makes three we've now found."

Jasmine rubbed her ring and visualized the camp and instantly appeared. She quickly told her grandmother what was going on and left the egg with her and quickly returned back to Melody, who was still standing where she had been when she left and looked startled when Jasmine appeared again.

"Oh, Jasmine, you scared me."

"I'm sorry. Melody, this ring works so fast that I get caught up in traveling at such a high speed that it leaves me feeling dizzy. Wait for a moment, and then we'll go and get the eggs. I brought Philo back with me."

Valley of the Yellow Stones

Chapter Thirteen ☼
Philo

Melody and Jasmine hurried to the storeroom, snuck over to the box, and saw that the chain had been removed. Melody quickly opened it and grabbed an egg while Jasmine took Philo out of her pouch and placed her on the floor and told her to get an egg. She did. Suddenly, they heard a guard coming, and Melody handed the egg to Jasmine and when she put it in her pouch, Melody ran over to hide in the closet. Jasmine hurried out the side door and went down the west hall leading outside. She looked around, ran over to the oak tree, sat down, and waited. Twenty minutes later, she saw the guard come out of the temple, and waited until he turned and started down the path leading to the forest. She then hurried back in to the temple, quietly went into the storage room and saw Melody standing with a shocked expression. She looked down on the floor and saw little Philo's body with blood coming from his mouth.

Oh, Melody, what happened? How did Phil…Philo get…Oh!" She cried as she leaned down and picked him up and held him close to her chest while crying.

Melody said, "He fought for you and help save your life."

"What are you talking about?"

"The guard saw you and started to go after you when Philo jumped on him and bite him. The guard hit him on the head with his sword. He was a loyal friend, Jasmine."

"Oh Melody, my heart is so heavy that I want to go kill the guard myself. This is a day of mourning, so I won't, but one day…one day…Oh, I just want to go back to camp. Let's go Melody."

"Yes, let's go to camp, Jasmine."

Jasmine wrapped Philo with her scarf, and then placed her in the pouch and they left.

When they returned Ramara was sleeping, but when she heard Jasmine and Melody arrive, she sat up and looked shocked at Jasmine as she laid Philo on the tree stump and cried, "I've lost you. Oh, Philo, my baby, who will snuggle with me, now? It will never be the same without you."

Ramara got up and went to her granddaughter and held her closely to her chest and said, "Granddaughter, we will put her on the wagon and take her to the Crystal City where the priest will bury her in the garden."

"Yes, Granddaughter, we will prepare for the journey immediately and we will take these two golden eggs. That makes five we've found. Soon, we will return to our village and take them there for our weather conditions to brighten."

"Yes, Grandmother, I'll prepare for our journey. It is a sad day and traveling will do me good." She turned to Melody and said, "Tell the men when they return where we went and will be back soon.

"Yes, I will Jasmine."

As they laid Philo in a wooden box, Jazzell and Cosmos were making crying sounds and continued to touch Philo until Ramara removed them and put them in Jasmine's pouch and handed it to her. All loaded up, they galloped away toward Crystal City.

Soon upon arriving at Crystal City, Jasmine paused a while and looked at the pyramid temple in the coolness of the day. Then she climbed off Breezy and moved with her grandmother to the steps and began climbing to the top of the temple's entrance. The large wooden doors with the Tree of Life attached to it no longer thrilled her as it had before. She didn't stand in awe, but she opened the doors and entered with a heavy heart as she held Philo in her arms. Ramara walked beside her carrying the two golden eggs.

Almost immediately a priest approached them and noticed right away that Jasmine was distressed. He took Philo into his arms and they walked without saying a word and then he placed Philo on the altar, and they sat beside him on each side while Ramara spoke with the high priest about the eggs. The priest spoke softly, and then chanted for a moment before he took Philo outside, and had another priest bury him in the garden beside the weeping willow tree. The two of them, then sat on the stone bench as the priest told Jasmine that she must accept the fact that it was Philo's time to leave earth and to move on to another place. She turned to the priest with tears in her eyes and said, "I know, but my heart is heavy."

"I know child, but you will soon pass through this loss, and then you will see clearer that you will be fine without Philo. You see we all have a certain amount of time when we come to earth, and when it is up, we sweetly allow the tears of loss to come and then we wipe them and smile while getting on with our adventures here on earth."

"High Priest, I accept your wisdom, and will let my tears flow for a day, and then I will smile as you say and continue on with my life with a smile upon my face."

He touched her hand and said, "You are wise my child. You still have a lot to accomplish and I know you will. Now go and leave Philo with me. I shall visit him under this willow tree every day to help him make his transformation into his next place."

Ramara was standing in the doorway as they entered, and the priest said, "Ramara, it is time for you to rest. You must go to the grounds of relaxation and spend the rest of your days in peace. These wars are not for an old woman, even a shaman at that. You've served your people long enough."

"High Priest, you are a wise saint. I intend to go when the sun rises 10 more times."

"Very well, then I bid you farewell, and send you off with these special seeds to grow in your village Jasmine. When they begin to grow, you make sure you speak to them as you would to a child, and they will listen to you and serve you well. These seeds are magical, Jasmine."

As they climbed on their horses, the priest waved to them until they could no longer see him standing.

Philo

Chapter Fourteen ☼

Water of Forgetfulness

Ivan, Melody, and the men have been traveling all day without any rest or food. They came across a brook with a pool of cool water, and it was so inviting that they stopped to indulge themselves.

The entire army was so tired and thirsty; they ran to the water and drank until their bellies were filled. Soon after, they didn't even know where they were or who anyone around were. Melody demanded they rest and eat something. They didn't have food, but she was sure if they went into the forest, they could find something to make for dinner. The horses and oxen were dazed and walking as if they were drunk or lost. Ivan could barely speak, but he forced himself to say hoarsely, "Men get away from the water and rest. It is causing us a loss of memory. We need to rest and find food."

The men couldn't speak, but they slowly moved away from the water and fell to the ground in confusion. Everything looked fuzzy, and they couldn't remember who they were. Melody watched in horror and then lifted her arms up to the heavens and bellowed out, "Give these men rest and then fill them with memory."

Ivan went to the water and stood beside her and couldn't remember who she was, but bellowed out, "Water, water in the pond of dreams, tell me what is in your curse that makes men dream."

The water started to swell, and, in its churning, it rose high, and on top of the bubbling water sat a lady with long golden hair. Half of her body was a woman, and the other half was a fish. She said, "Who called the water of forgetfulness."

"It is I," said, Melody. What curse have you put on these men and our animals".

"Those who drink of the water of forgetfulness will not remember forever." The water lady said.

"What can be done to remove the curse of forgetfulness?" Melody asked.

"It is the curse of the water spirit because too many were putting bad things into the water and killing the fish and plants. They would not listen to the spirits of the water. So, they cursed it and whoever drinks will forget."

"We come in peace and only came for a cool drink; not to dirty the water. Why must we be cursed?" Melody said.

"If you speak truth then go to Raphael, a place to the north where you can get the curse removed. If you speak truth to the Infinite Knowledgeable Salmon Fish, he will know and then free your men of forgetfulness. Go to the waterfall, there you will find the sacred pond. It is encircled by nine hazelnut trees. Infinite Salmon Fish lives in the pond and has infinite knowledge. The Queen will take you to Salmon Fish Raphael, and then you must ask for the curse to be broken."

Melody told Ivan and the men to rest and not to leave the campground. "I'm riding over to get Jasmine. I know she will be able to help me get you all to Raphael. She climbed on her horse and raced away toward Ramara and Jasmine's campsite.

Soon upon arriving she saw Ramara and Jasmine sitting near the fire. "Jasmine! Jasmine! Please come with me. Ivan and the men drink from the forgetful pond, and now they can't remember anything, nor do they know anyone."

Jasmine jumped up and said, "Wait! I must get my stone. I'll leave Grandmother here because we just got back from the temple and she's mighty tired."

"Hurry! I'm concerned Ivan and the men won't remember to wait at the brook for me."

Jasmine whistled for Breezy, and he came running, and she jumped on his back and off she went, following Melody down the dirt path.

Ivan and the men had been so tired that they were snoring over near the oak tree. Jasmine got off Breezy and ran over to Ivan and started shaking him. "Ivan! Ivan! Wake up. We need to take you to Maxo."

Ivan raised his head and looked at Jasmine with a strange look about him, "What? Who are you? What do you want?"

"Oh Ivan, it's me, Jasmine. Please remember…remember me."

Ivan shook his head and said, "Am I supposed to know you?"

Jasmine turned her head away and let out a sigh and said, "It's okay Ivan. Get up! I'm taking you to Maxo."

Melody had everything loaded up and ready by the time Jasmine finally had Ivan on his horse. After riding for what seemed like hours, they got off their horses and walked the rest of the way with their horses walking beside them. As they got closer to the pond, they could see the nine hazelnut trees just as the Lady of Forgetfulness had said. They walked to the sandy shoreline and instantly saw Queen Maxo. She walked over to them all and said, "What brings you here?"

"Lady of Forgetfulness said you could help us. You see we drank from the forgetful waters, but we didn't do anything but drink."

"I see. Humm, well, follow me, and I'll take you to Salmon Fish."

They all stood in front of the pond and saw that it was beautiful and full of energy with the water sparkling like crystals in its blueness. The sun was shimmering on the water and sent prisms across the pond looking like precious gems.

"Salmon Fish rise up! We have people here who claim to speak truth about not littering the brook. Show yourself and tell me if they do indeed speak truth." The Queen said and then turned to look at the men.

Jasmine became impatient and said, "Salmon Fish rise up!

We need your help."

But the pond was still and at first, they thought there wasn't anything in the water because it was so clear, and they could see the bottom. Suddenly, big waves started to swirl around and around and up popped Salmon Fish's head. "What is it" You call upon me on such a beautiful day when I am in a state of bliss."

"Hello, Raphael infinite knowledgeable fish. I'm Jasmine, granddaughter of Ramara, the shaman of the Valley of the Yellow Stones. We come asking you to release the curse of the water of forgetfulness. We came in peace, only to drink the brook's dampness. Won't you please release the curse?"

"I see. Then what would you do for me if I release the curse?"

"We would promise never to put anything harmful into the brook." Jasmine said.

"Jasmine, you speak truth. You are wise beyond your years, and for this, I say, release the curse! Go! Go to the hazelnut tree and pick up the hazelnuts that have fallen; only the ones on the ground because they hold magic. Give each one who drank the water of forgetfulness. That is all. Go! Leave me to my blissful day." Raphael Salmon Fish said, and the water began to swirl around and around in the blueness of the pond and then a big splash and Salmon Fish was gone.

After eating the hazelnut, memory was returned to all those who drank the water.

Chapter Fifteen ☼

Another Sacred Golden Egg Retrieved

Jasmine received word that in the town of Gaelan a secret message awaited her. She needed to go immediately, but Breezy had stepped on a stone and bruised her hoof. Knowing it needed to heal before riding him, she paced back and forth deciding how to get to Gaelan. Ruddey saw Jasmine pacing and thinking so he said, "I can fly you to Gaelan, Jasmine, that is, if you trust me."

What a ruckus that created. Hickey right away shouted, "No."

Melody said, "I'm not sure that's a good idea, Jasmine."

While Jasmine was wondering what to do, Ruddey said, "I promise I won't blow any fire your way."

Hickey spoke up, "Well, if he goes, I have to go too. Someone needs to watch out for the old heat blower."

"Oh, Hickey, you don't need to watch over me. After all, I'm so much bigger than you."

"No Ruddey, I'm going to, bigger or not. No telling what trouble you will get into if I'm not there to remind you to behave yourself. You're such a whiner."

Jasmine smiled as she snickered under her breath. They seem always to make her laugh.

With Ivan in the forest and Ramara's horse was tired from the day's journey, she said, "Okay Ruddey, let's do it, and Hickey you may go too."

Melody looked in puzzlement at Ramara and said, "Is she crazy? I wouldn't be caught dead riding on that dragon. No! He'd end up killing me or no telling where he'd land Jasmine.

No doubt in a berry patch." She chuckled and went over to Ramara and handed her an apple.

"Don't fret so Melody; Jasmine knows what she's doing."

"Thank you, Grandmother,"

"Okay, Ramara, I suspect you're right," Melody said as she sat down on the ground and began wrapping string around her bedding.

"I made this wreath of Garlic, Granddaughter," Ramara said as she wrapped it around Ruddey's neck. "I bid thy power to be yours for an hour and to make you strong, not weak. It will give you wisdom and courage not to flee. Thy will be done. Let it be!"

Ruddey's chest pumped up and out came a huge ball of fire from his mouth, and immediately he started coughing, and as he tried to catch his breath. "Oh, I got something caught in my throat; water please."

"A fine dragon you turned out to be." Hickey moaned, "Do you always have to blow fire when you cough? You big old clumsy dragon; what am I going to do with you?"

"It is because I have a sore throat," said Ruddey.

"Huff, you always have a sore throat." Hickey groaned.

"I'm helping Jasmine, Hickey. Helping is a good thing anyway. Ivan said there is always something good about helping humanity. I cannot at present describe it," said Ruddey.

"Oh, you wacky dragon, he was talking about having to fight those who are invading villages and killing just for their entertainment," said Hickey.

"Enough!" shouted Jasmine.

"This is madness!" Melody bellowed out. "Perhaps this isn't a good idea after all!"

"Be on your way, Jasmine. Be gone and stop complaining Hickey," Ramara said with authority in her voice.

Jasmine and Hickey hopped up on Ruddey and off they went; a little tipsy on the takeoff, but after a few minutes he straightened out, and you could hear Hickey yelling, "Turn left you over-stuffed dragon. Go left!"

They disappeared under the stars and into the night. It didn't take them long, and they were at the Gaelan gates when Ruddey tried to land by the wall of the town, but instead skid down the hill. Trying to put on his breaks, he instead hit the wall hard. "Ohhh, I'm not used to carrying anyone."

Jasmine was holding on for dear life. "That was sure a wild ride there, Ruddey." Jasmine said as she leaped off trying to compose herself.

"Can't you ever glide in when you land and stay on your feet? Hickey shouted as she barely hung on to a tree branch.

Jasmine said, "Now Rudy don't forget the garlic wreath will give you courage." She gave Rudy a kiss on the cheek and said, "This is for luck."

Ruddey turned red and said, "Ayah" He touched his cheek with his wing as if to say*, I'll never wash my face again.*

Hickey said, "okay you big beast get over it because we've got work to do."

Jasmine said, "You stay here at the gate Ruddey, and be as quiet as you can be. Do you think you can do that Ruddey?"

"Oh yes," he said as he started walking backwards toward the grove of trees stepping on the branches and making noise.

"Be quiet!" Hickey whispered. "Don't you know what quiet means?"

Ruddey said, "I am sorry I didn't see the dead branches," and then tip-toed into the Forest and out of sight so no one would see him.

"We will meet you here in an hour."

Jasmine and Hickey walked nervously through the gates and down the street to the Captain's Tavern where the message was to be waiting for Jasmine. Right away she noticed a group of men standing while drinking ale from wooden cups and out of the corner of one of the men's eye he saw them and yelled, "Come here woman!"

"I can't, you see I'm meeting my big brother around the corner and I'm already late."

The man waved for her to go on by and Jasmine breathed in a deep breath and then blew it out relieved.

"That was close. Whew." Hickey said as she looked at the large building that was dark and uninviting. "This doesn't look good."

"Listen, Hickey, I don't know what we're getting ourselves into so be alert," Jasmine said as they walked closer to the side of the building and saw right away a courtyard. There in the middle set a tall Brigid Goddess sculpture of the three sisters which represent wisdom, guidance, and prophecy.

"Oh, look! Melody, the Brigid Goddess. I've heard so much about that statue but never seen it until now. Melody did you know, it's a midwife healer; lady blacksmith with an anvil which represents the keeper of the fire." Jasmine walked over to it and looked intently at it and then placed her hand on it and said to the sculpture, "I humbly ask with an open heart and mind that my truth will find me."

Several moments passed then a creaking and breaking sound came from the wall which made Jasmine step back in fear it was crumbling right there in front of her. The Wall opened, and she saw two big turquoise eyes looking at her.

"Ohh, you startled me. I'm Jasmine, the granddaughter of Ramara, daughter of Cetus. I have come a long way from the Valley of the Yellow Stones. Do you have a message for me?" I'm hoping you know where the rest of our Sacred Golden Eggs of our temple are."

"I'm Negal of the wall. I am the messenger of all who comes to seek my guidance. I do have a message for you that will guide you to one of the sacred eggs."Volga Temple is where it is setting; on an altar. There are guards all around the square protecting it, so you'll have to go in through the roof where it opens to the inside ceiling over the altar. There it is exposed to the moon and sun. The light from the moon and sun will guide you; the light shines directly over the egg sitting on the altar."

"You have been most helpful Negal. Thank you."

"One more thing," said Negal, "It is you that is to retrieve the sacred egg, right? I sense a bad outcome with that clumsy old dragon you came on; possibly falling through the ceiling and alerting the guards. May God be with you dear child."

Jasmine bowed her head as Negal left them and the wall slowly closed.

Right away Jasmine went to the Volga Temple and looked through the open door and saw the golden egg sitting on the altar just as Negal had said. She could see it sparkle in its goldenness and at that moment began to make her plan to retrieve it. She looked up and knew Negal spoke truth; the ceiling door was open.

Jasmine whispered to Hickey who was sitting on her shoulder, "We need to go get Ruddey, before the lackluster celebrant returns. Negal said he would be gone for a couple of hours."

Hickey frowned, looking puzzled and said, "Why on earth would you need Ruddey?"

"He is going to retrieve the sacred egg."

"You've got to be kidding!" said Hickey.

"No, we need him."

Hickey shook her head in bafflement and said, "This is really going to be a good one! I hope he doesn't sneeze and blow up the temple!"

"Have faith Hickey. I know what I'm doing."

Jasmine and Hickey hurried back to the town's gate, and Jasmine called out to Rudy, but he didn't come. She walked a little further into the tree grove, gave another yell and this time she heard some leaves wrestling. Jasmine woke him and Hickey said, "Rudy this is not the time to be sleeping on the job. We've got work to do you snoring old coot!"

Jasmine told Ruddey he was going to swoop down and grab

the egg and become a *champion egg hero*.

"Now Ruddey don't forget to meet me at the gate to pick us up and then you'll fly us back to camp."

"I can't do that! What if I lose the egg?"

"You won't. I have all the faith in the world, you'll do just fine."

"Ohh, won't you do it for me?"

"No, but I will give you another kiss for luck if you do it, plus don't forget that you have the garlic wreath around your neck for protection," Jasmine said as she smiled.

Hickey groaned and then said, "Ruddey, you know how much the eggs mean to the people of the valley."

"Yes, I do. Oh yeah, that humanity thing Ivan spoke about. Okay, I have people depending on me; I'll do it."

"I'll go with him and make sure he doesn't mess things up, Jasmine."

Jasmine gave Ruddey a hug and a big kiss, and she chuckled when she saw it made Ruddey's whole body turn red.

"For humanity, I know I can do this," Ruddey said as his redness began to fade.

"Yes, you can, and you'll make me proud of you."

Ruddey left with Hickey riding on him, and as they turned the corner, Jasmine bellowed out, "Good luck Ruddey!"

Ruddey flapped his wings harder and off they went, going higher and higher up into the sky. The whole town looked up in awe at him. Jasmine chuckled because she could see that Hickey was directing Ruddey like a traffic director. They circled two times, and then he dove down straight into the courtyard down in through the opening. He grabbed the egg and flew up into the air with Hickey.

The soldiers saw him and threw spears and drew back their bows and shot arrows, but always missing him. He made another swoop feeling fairly proud of himself; so much that he blew out and a hot fire shot down at the soldiers, making them run for cover. One of the soldiers shot an arrow and when it was going to hit Hickey, Ruddey quickly and just in time turned and it hit Ruddey in his leg.

"Oh, my, oh my, Ruddey, you saved my life!" Hickey cried.

Just as Ruddey arrived back to Jasmine, he got a sharp pain in his foot and accidentally let go of the egg.

Hickey said, "Now you done it! I knew it! You did it again, didn't you? Ugh! I have to do everything!"

"I'm sorry." Ruddey moaned.

"You go ahead. Go to Jasmine. I'll fly back and get the egg."

"Oh, Hickey, I'm so sorry."

"Do as I say; go! I will get it."

Rudy flew back to the gate and Hickey flew off, and right away she saw the egg setting nicely on a roof of an old house. Smoke was coming out of the chimney and it was dreadful to Hickey's eyes. She rubbed and rubbed them to stop the burning, but she was still able to rescue the egg.

"I've got it! Let's get out of here!"

The three of them were excited about finding another egg and were laughing so hard that they almost missed their landing area. But they made it nonetheless right in front of Ramara who was waiting for them.

Soon as they landed, Ramara saw the arrow in Ruddey's leg and quickly ran to get her herb and immediately mixed it with cloves and other spices and applied it to his leg.

When Ramara was almost finished bandaging Ruddey, Hickey swayed up to Ruddey and said, "Old friend, you saved my life this very night. I will never forget. I've been hard on you these past years." She sprinkled stardust on his leg and said, "I love you Ruddey. You are my very best friend."

"Ohh Hickey, you love me! We're friends through thick and thin; forever!"

Ruddey, Jasmine, and Hickey sat down near the fire and began telling their impressive story to Ramara. The men began to cheer, and Jasmine said, "Ruddey really did have courage and he saved Hickey's life and brought back another sacred egg. He's a *champion egg hero*."

"We now have retrieved three eggs!" Ramara smiled as she put Cosmos down on the ground to run around before bedding down.

Chapter Sixteen ☼

Ramara, the Story Teller

Ramara loved to tell stories so that night before bedding down, she began telling Melody, Jasmine, Ruddey, and Hickey the one about the Green Woman.

She began by saying; the mountain stream snaked its way through the tightly growing trees as Green Woman smiled at the gushing and bubbling of the steam while it flowed in its downward path over grey granite rocks heading to the valley below. That day she had dropped on one knee and swiftly moved her bundle of hand-picked berries around until the rushing water cleaned them to a sparkle. She was the spirit of the trees; her eyes twinkled like stars, and her soul paraded through her body like a gem. They say her clothing was made from the trees. She wore feathers and vines around her wrists and ankles. Her long green wavy hair that ended at her waist would blow away from her face in the furious winds; looking like a tree limb.

Green Woman has seen many sunsets upon the branches and roots while being doused with enchanting rain. Her powers and service to the earth were to help people, animals and nature. Never a day went by without her giving her praises to mother earth in her wonderful divine goodness to shower her beauty to all. She spoke to all who would listen of the earth's wisdom, always giving in abundance and sprinkled them with light and blessings.

Often, she would help people to master water and the beings of water through feelings and magnetism of their emotions; manifesting through the psychical plane. Ramara stopped and put Cosmos to bed and finished her story. "You see emotions are necessary to bring changes upon the earth. You know like water gushing over rocks which by the way relieve traumatic memory from beginning to end. Genavive of the Mountains once told a story about a little bird that was the most beautiful colorful bird of all other birds in the forest. There wasn't any other like its kind. Little bird flew far away deep into the forest and became frightened because he realized he was lost and trying to scurry around to find his way, he hurt his wing, which didn't make his fears any better and winter was coming so he knew he had to find a safe warm place to land. Little bird went to the birch tree and looked at it and said, "Ohh, I don't want to stay on this branch because they are too small and might not hold me. He hurried over to a mighty oak tree, and the oak tree said, "Won't you stay with me for I have acorns and you can eat all you want."

Little bird said, "Oh, no I don't like acorns." The little bird of many colors went to another tree, and the tree wanted the bird to stay and set on his limbs, but little bird of many colors said, "I don't know what kind of tree you are, so no, I can't stay with you."

Finally, little bird of many colors came upon a raggedy old pine tree that wasn't pretty because someone had cut some of his branches, but the pine tree had such a wonderful soft voice when he offered little bird to stay and set upon his limbs. He said, "I have strong branches and the juniper tree next to me can protect you from the north wind and it has tasty berries for you to eat. Around here we take care of those in need and you have a hurt wing so please land down on my branch and stay for the winter.

Little bird of many colors said, "I do have a hurt wing, and it's difficult for me to fly around and fend for myself without shelter."

"Then little bird land on my branch and make yourself comfortable. I can warm you if you get close to my trunk."

Little bird looked sad, and his wing hurt. He said, "I have a

hurt wing and would need to stay till winter's end. I haven't shelter, and I'm mighty cold and hungry."
The pine tree said, "Of course you may stay with me till winter's end."

The little bird didn't know what else he could do. He felt all alone, cold, and his wing was hurting from all the flying around trying to find warmth. He said, "I wouldn't disturb your branches, would I? I think I would like to stay for the winter's end with you."

"Well then, come right here and live on my strong branches, over here close to my truck to keep you warm," said the warm pine tree.

"Oh, pine tree, you are a gracious tree."

"Little bird you can stay as long as you wish."

"Oh, pine tree your heart is big."

"Little bird, come and get warm in my tree."

The juniper tree that set next to the pine tree told the little bird when the cold winds come, I will protect you from the cold coming in from the north.

"I can help too." Another tree said, "I have small berries that are small and tasty."

Little bird landed on a limb in the pine tree and snuggled up close to the trunk and soon fell asleep."

The next couple of weeks all the beautiful leaves lay on the ground from the cold winds coming in and every leaf that the wind touched, more fell to the ground.

The wind looked down on all the trees and realized if she blew on the juniper, pine and spruce tree, she would have the Green Woman's spirit to attend to. She knew it would harm the little bird, so she didn't blow her wind near those three trees.

Ramara looked over to the ones listening intently to her story and said, "That's why those trees keep their leaves in the winter; to help protect little birds."

"Ramara you are the best storyteller around," said Ivan as he climbed off his horse and walked over near the fire. He looked tired and right away Jasmine's heart started beating fast and hard.

Chapter Seventeen ☼

The trip to the Vikon Mountain

Ivan went over to the wooden bowl, washed his face, and then sat down beside Jasmine. “How’s the best warrior I’ve ever fought back to back with?

Jasmine looked up into Ivan’s eyes and smiled. “I’m happy to see you; that’s how this warrior is.”

With those words, Cosmos rounded himself up still more snugly than before, gave a squeaky grunt and went back to dream-world where he was dreaming of Philo. He missed Philo and often felt good after dreaming of him in playful dream times.

Ivan right away became paralyzed with shyness and sat blushing at the ground, unable to respond to Jasmine’s words. She chuckled to herself as she scooted over closer to him and whispered, “Did you lose your tongue to speak?”

Past the shy stage, he turned to her and lifted her hand to his mouth and kissed it, “Only for a moment.”

“I’m glad it lasted for only a moment,” Jasmine smiled mischievously.

Ivan chuckled and then said, “So, three of the eggs are retrieved, and that means we have ten more to go. I suggest come morning we go back to the Vikon temple and search for them.”

“Yes, I’d like that. Perhaps we should leave Grandmother here, she’s been fairly tired lately, in fact, just yesterday she mentioned we should go back to our village and see how my brother, Hardon is doing with the rebuilding.”

“Okay, we’ll go at the first sunrise to Vikon Mountain and then return back here to take her to the Valley of the Yellow Stones.”

The next morning the men loaded up for Jasmine and Ivan. Melody decided to stay with Ramara, but Ruddey and Hickey asked to join them.

"Jasmine, I checked Breezy's hoofs and think she needs another day for her bruises to heal so why don't you ride on your grandmother's horse. He's fast and will not fail you."

By mid-morning, they headed toward Vikon Mountain and soon after arriving about a mile within the area they stopped to rest and discuss their plan.

"I think the men and I should go in first and check things out and then when you hear my whistle; one long and two short ones, you come in with Ruddey and Hickey."

Ivan took two of his men while the others waited just outside the area near the stream and walked in through the open gate. It was quiet and it didn't seem any Vikons were near the temple, but he wanted to be sure before he whistled for Jasmine, so he walked up closer to the temple and saw two guards drinking ale from a wooden cup. He whispered to his two men and told them to go tie them up and throw them in the nearby well.

The sloped courtyard was long with a sandy passage leading up to the temple. It had a covered passage immediately before the massive doors and Ivan saw his two men come in from both sides; one man signaled to the other and then they swiftly ran and attacked both guards at the same time while placing a hand over each guard's mouth in order to keep them quiet. After knocking them out, they tied them and threw them into the well. Ivan stood for a moment longer to make sure there weren't any more guards, and when he felt secure in his observations, he let out his long whistle and then two shorts ones.

Jasmine came immediately riding on Ruddey with Hickey on her shoulder. They stopped at once when they saw Ivan motioning for them to hide behind the tree. Jasmine got off Ruddey stepped behind the tree and waited for Ivan to give them further instructions. A man appeared from the temple and walked over to Ivan. “Who are you?” asked the man. “Tell me who you are before I have to call on my men.”

“I’m a wandering man who has lost his mind, looking for my wife. Have you seen her?” Ivan quickly responded.

“How would I know who your wife is? I’ve not seen any woman in weeks. My men have not returned, and I was just about to go searching for them. If you come along with me, I shall help you find your lost woman.”

“I will, but first I have to sleep for an hour, tell me in what direction you are headed, and I shall come directly afterward. I have a fast horse, and I’m sure he will catch up with you before you go far.” Ivan said in a convincing voice.

“Very well, but don’t take long.”

The man got on his horse which looked like he hadn’t eaten in a week and slowly headed toward the sandy path leading out the gate. Jasmine moved around to the other side of the tree when she saw the man approaching and motioned for Ruddey to be still. Hickey placed her two fingers over her mouth at Ruddey to make sure he was quiet. The man passed without seeing them and started talking to himself as he rode out into the forest.

With Ivan’s signal, the three hurried over to Ivan. Jasmine commanded Ruddey and Hickey to wait outside to keep guard while they went inside.

“I’m the *hero,* so I will pay close attention and alert you if someone comes,” Ruddey said looking proud.

“I will stay and make sure he does,” said Hickey.

“I’m the hero Hickey. But I’ll let you.”

“Before you drive me mad Ruddey, hush up!” Hickey said strongly.

Jasmine said, “Shhh…you two. We’ll be right back.”

Once inside the temple, in the storage room of the west wing, Ivan said, “It looks as if all the Vikons are gone. We must have killed more in war than we thought.”

Jasmine smiled and said, “I know we did.”

Over near the window sat the box, but when Jasmine opened it, all the eggs were gone. “Oh, no! They’re gone!” cried Jasmine.

“They must be here somewhere, keep looking.” Ivan groaned.

They searched the whole room but found nothing and about the time they were going to go into another room they heard Ruddey screaming loudly. They ran outside as quickly as they could go and instantly saw the most beautiful site they ever imagined. Ruddey had two golden eggs in his hand and Hickey had a small basket with two inside.

“Oh, where did you find the eggs?” Jasmine said while Ivan took the two from Ruddey and put them into the basket Hickey was holding and took it and said, “Hickey you ride on Ruddey’s back and Ruddey you hurry back to camp and leave these with Ramara and come back here.”

“We found them buried in that bush,” said Hickey. “Okay we’ll go and come directly back.”

“Yes, I saw the fresh soil lumpy and knew something was buried there,” Ruddey said.

“You did not! I pointed to it and you dug it up,” shouted Hickey.

“Go! Go you two. Someone might still be here,” Ivan groaned.

As soon as Ruddey and Hickey left, Jasmine told Ivan to go look under all the trees that were close to the temple. She looked all around the temple to see if there were any boxes or containers, but there weren’t any, so she went out to the last tree Ivan was searching, but again, nothing. They decided to go back in the temple just as Ruddey and Hickey had returned, so the four of them went into the temple to search, but again, nothing.

They decided to go back to camp and Jasmine mentioned something about asking for guidance from Bevin of the Lake or Consa, but they both decided it would have to be after they returned from Valley of the Yellow Stones.

Chapter Eighteen ☼

The Return to Valley of the Yellow Stones

Everybody had started for the Valley of the Yellow Stones, and when they arrived the village was empty which troubled Ramara. She looked around and saw that the temple had been rebuilt, but nothing else. There were tents up, and it looked as if they had all left in a hurry because a fire was still burning in the pit where they had cooked wild turkey.

"Where did everybody go?" Jasmine asked

"I'm concerned Granddaughter. Something is not right here."

"Ramara," Ivan said reasonably, "I think you should go inside the temple and rest while the rest of us go out to see what is going on."

Ruddey spoke up concerned, "Me too?"

"No, not you too… you big…oh, whatever!" Hickey mumbled as she looked around and felt sadness.

"No, Ruddey, you and Hickey stay right outside the temple." Ivan said as he turned to Jasmine and said, "Let's go."

They rode side by side looking to the east and then the west, riding over hills down in the valley and over to the stream and that's where they saw all the village men and women standing over what looked like a grave. "Oh my God, someone is being buried. Oh Goodness!" Jasmine cried as she got off Breezy and ran over to the village people and said, "Who?"

Her brother, Morred, looked down at her and cried, "It's

our brother, Hardon. The Vikons came into the village two weeks after you and Grandmother left, and he tried to stop them from taking one of our women and the Vikon killed him and took Suesue anyway. Other villages came to help build the Temple, but no one had the heart to do anymore. Each day, we come here to Hardon's grave and ask for guidance, but we never get an answer. Right before he died, he mumbled something about he'd still guide us to the end, but apparently he can't because he never answers us."

Tears began running down Jasmine's face as she turned to Ivan and he took her into his arms and whispered, "We'll build the village Jasmine. I'm sorry about your brother."

"Yes, we will, and we will go get the sacred eggs the priest is holding for us at the Crystal Temple. We need them for our Solstice and Equinox. Even without all of them, we will be able to protect the weather conditions to a great extent. Hardon would have wanted that."

"Very well. But for now, let's go back and put together a plan for the building of the village." He turned to Morred and asked, "Who is the new the Magistrate?"

"I am. We all voted. Without Ramara here we didn't know what to do, but in the long run, decided to go ahead and vote."

Ivan patted Morred on the back and said, "You did well. Meet us back at the village, and we'll talk with Ramara about rebuilding the village."

"Ivan, the decision is Morred's, now that he's the Magistrate, but Grandmother would love to see you Morred."

"It's okay, Jasmine, I think Ivan's help would be fine. I've heard about you all over the land, Ivan. Please be of assistance in our village." Morred said and then turn to the village people and said, "People journey back to the temple, we have things to discuss, but Saul, you go to the neighboring two villages and tell them to attend our meeting at once."

"Yes, I will, Morred."

Chapter Nineteen ☼

Ivan's Farm and the Rebuilding of the Valley of the Yellow Stones

Soon upon arriving back to the village, Ramara ran to Ivan and said, "Ivan, your brother is here and says it's urgent he speak with you. Come and I'll take you to him."

As Ivan walked into the library of the temple, he saw his brother, standing and looking at the wall of gold plates the village's people made for display.

Joseph turned around and saw Ivan and moved quickly over to him, "Ivan we've been looking for you all over the land. I have married and I'm asking you to put the farm in my name alone since you are no longer working on it. I shall offer you coins for your part and help you in any way I can."

"Come here brother, closer to me, so I can hug you." As they hugged Ivan whispered in his ear, "The farm is yours without coins, but I will request something of you; to send your village men to help rebuild this destroyed village."

It was agreed upon immediately and Joseph returned back to his farm to get his village's men to help rebuild the Valley of the Yellow Stones.

After their meeting, they drank wine and sat under the stars, enjoying the last of the hot flame of their camp fire before retiring for the night. The huts were skimpy and shabby, compared with the splendid ones they had before the fire destroyed the village, but it was enough to give them privacy and warmth. Everybody had gone to bed except Jasmine and Ivan. They decided to go for a long walk and bath before going to bed. Ivan wouldn't allow Jasmine to go without him until he knew there were no longer Vikons in the area, so she accepted his offer and he promised to turn his back until she was finished bathing. Afterward they walked back hand in hand as they laughed about Ivan falling in the water when he tried to back up from a snake near the water. Then before she went into her own tent, Ivan put his arm around her and lightly kissed her on the nose and said, “Good night Jasmine.”

The next morning as Ivan was eating his morning berries, he heard hoofs coming hard and fast; sounding like thunder. He looked up and hundreds of men riding on their horses with carts behind them carrying wood and other material for the rebuilding of the village. He jumped up and shouted, “The men are here, to rebuild. Get up men! Get up Ramara! Get up Jasmine!” He went to each tent and slapped it hard and then threw more wood in the fire laughing out loud like Jasmine had never heard before. She quickly dressed and stepped out of her tent and saw him overjoyed. She ran to him and wrapped her arms around him, and they danced as the men rode into the village.

Within the hour the reconstruction of the village started going up faster than anyone imagined. Ruddey and Hickey were even helping and believe it or not, they were getting along. Ramara told them if they were great helpers, she’d tell them another story later that night while they drank their wine and celebrated the new construction.

When the stars came out and the men drank their wine in wooden cups overflowing, Ruddey said, “Ramara’s going to tell us a story. Hurry Hickey! Hurry and set by me. You can even lie on my back while you listen.”

Ramara chuckled as she threw another log in the fire before she sat down to begin her story. She felt better already being back in her village and wondered whether she should stay another year before retiring in Consa’s Secret Garden.

“Okay Ruddey get settled because I’m about to keep my promise to you and Hickey.”

“We’re ready Ramara. We’re ready! See! We’re cozy and

waiting."
"Well then, let me begin."
There was a young lad who had a bad temper and it cost him more wasted time and loss of good friends than any other ingredient in his life. He approached an old wise man who was wearing rags and asked, "Old man, how can I get control of these temper demons of rage that covet me?"

The old man told the lad to position himself at a waterless hideaway far off in the dry land and sit there among trees and draw up the briny water for any traveler who might venture there."

The lad, wanting to conquer his bad temper and rage, rode out to the desert near some withered trees. For months, he wore nothing but robes and face bands to guard his skin against the flying sand. He drew the tart water and gave it to all who drew near. Years passed and he suffered no more hysterics of temper.

One day a stranger came and gave the lad a grunt after he offered him water from a wooden cup. He scoffed at the foggy water and refused it; riding off.

Yes, you guessed it! The lad became enraged, so much that he was blinded by his next actions. He pulled the stranger down from his camel and executed him. He of course became grieved that he had allowed himself to be consumed by rage. He lowered his head in shame.

Suddenly, up rode another stranger. He looked at the dead man and said, "Thank you young lad. Thank you. You have killed the man who was on his way to murder the king!"

Within minutes, the foggy water turned clear and sweet and the withered trees blushed green and burst into joyous bloom.

"Oh Grandmother, you've told me that story before and I remember you telling me that when I was a small child; It's a teaching about not unleashing anger arbitrarily, except at the right time."

"Of course, Granddaughter, the tale begins when the young

lad ached to rid himself of rage and anger, then gave out water, life, even under bad conditions in order to do so. The bottom line is there's a time for right anger. So, all you men who have used your anger on Vikons, in order to save women and children; know this – there is a time for right anger."

"Oh Ramara, you're the greatest story teller of all times. You make me want to help with the building tomorrow so I may hear another one of your stories." Melody said as she went over and hugged Ramara.

"Me too! Me too!" Ruddey shouted.

"I could fly the night away. I loved the story!" Hickey said.

Chapter Twenty ☼

Bevin, Lady of Lake Isabella

By the time the sun peeked over the mountain sending its brightness down on the village, Jasmine was up and ready to go with Ivan to see Bevin, Lady of Lake Isabella to request guidance on finding the rest of the Sacred Golden Eggs.

Melody and Ramara were going to the Crystal Temple to get the eggs they had left in the priest's safe protection. Melody promised she would stay with Ramara to help her conduct her responsibilities to the village until Jasmine and Ivan returned. Ramara had already told Jasmine she would be going to Consa's Secret Garden to retire; therefore, Jasmine would soon take her grandmother's place as the village's shaman.

Slowly and splendidly, the two stallion horses galloped side by side as they left the village in route of the Bevin of the Lake's castle. Ivan winked at Jasmine as she smiled at him and then had Breezy race ahead of him with her long hair flying in the wind. Ivan chuckled to himself as he watched her fly across the dirt path up the hill. She slowed down soon after reaching the top of the hill and then came to a stop and got off Breezy to take a sip of water from her bag. She watched Ivan gallop toward her and then get off Gallo and then walk toward her. Her heart felt as if it was on fire as his tall, slender body approached her. He pushed his hands through his thick, dark hair and smiled his half smile at her which sent her heart flaming with desire.

A bell tolled in the distance and Jasmine paused as she listened and then turned to Ivan. “Isn’t that the bell to the temple in Byron’s village?”

He shrugged his shoulders and then got up to look off into the distance but didn’t see any movement or action of any kind, so he turned back and suggested they continue on their journey. As the hour grew later, the bell continued to ring, so they raced to the village and when they arrived there, they saw several Vikons attacking the village. This worried Ivan because he hadn’t brought any men with them, so he knew he had to put together a plan, and fast.

The ground ran with blood, and the dead men dropped one after another from the ranks alike of Vikons and the village people. They had loaded up a catapult and were shooting rocks at the Vikons, knocking them down one by one. Men were locking spear by spear, helmet on helmet and man against man. It was a fierce fight and Ivan stayed off in the distance waiting while planning what to do. All of a sudden Jasmine ran ahead and lifted her sword high in the air and screamed, “Vikons will no longer come to kill and take children from villages.” She rubbed her ring and jumped off Breezy and screamed as she instantly stopped in her tracks. She held out her arms and the white spirit of a wolf came out from her chest and she leaped onto three Vikons the great white spirit wolf attacked their necks and jumped on several other Vikons until there were none left. Ivan stood in amazement as he saw the white spirit wolf fading and Jasmine re-appearing.

He ran to her and grabbed her as she was falling to the ground. “Jasmine! Jasmine! Are you alright?”

Jasmine looked big-eyed and weak; she couldn’t respond to Ivan. He pulled her to his chest and whispered, “You’ll be fine, Jasmine. Your strength will return.”

Within minutes Jasmine’s strength returned and she stood up and shouted, “I’ve done it, Ivan! I called on the spirit of the white wolf and he came out of my chest. Oh Ivan, what an experience. Grandmother told me I could do it and I did! She said bone by bone, hair by hair, wild woman comes back when you call upon her."

Nestled amongst the tree were two small children crying and holding on to one another. Ivan moved over to them and picked them up and held them tightly to his chest comforting them when their mother ran to them and held out her arms screaming, "Ross! Bempy! You're all right! You're all right!"

Jasmine had recognized the impossible, or what she thought was the impossible, but in only in the miasma of her fearful mind. She had come to see she was indeed shaman material. Her worries were over for she knew she was ready to step into her grandmother's role and become the shaman her grandmother had always said she was to be and one day would be. Her fears were over. It was okay for her grandmother to go to Consa's Secret Garden and retire. Her grandmother had taught her well.

Soon after reaching Bevin, Jasmine said, "I've come to you Consa to gain knowledge from you. There are still Sacred Golden Eggs missing and we need your visions to guide us to them. As you know the eggs count time; cycle of time. It's the revolutions of earth and tells of times in the ancient world which was called serpent of light. It causes cosmic events and keeps the earth from wobbling. It has powers of the orbits and moon which is called precession of the equinox."

"Yes, Jasmine I do know. I also know about the blue comet and the 13 Sacred Golden Eggs. The spirits of the ancient ones are in the Golden Eggs."

"Yes, Consa, those eggs are the pathways to knowledge. The Sacred Golden Egg ceremonies, at the end of time, souls will go into 13 bodies with combined knowledge and become whole again on the holiest of days."

"Now tell me dear, Jasmine, what knowledge do you seek from me?"

Jasmine stood up and walked over to the bench and lowered

her head and then up into Consa's eyes and said, "There are still some Sacred Golden Eggs out there, and I have no vision as to where they are. I'm hoping you can guide me."

"You must go out to the well, the wishing well as some here call it. You go and sit until you see images in the water, then and only then, do you request your need. Then you say; *all right then, so be it. And it is so.* and then you must turn and walk away knowing you will find your answer."

Ivan stood up and took Jasmine's hand and led her to the well. They stood and then sit and then stood and finally they sat down and watched the water and when Jasmine saw the image of a mountain top swirling around in the water she squealed out to Ivan, "See it? I saw a mountain top."

"I do too, but where?" Ivan said as he frowned.

"Well of your depth, please grant me a wish. I request and I need to find the rest of Valley of the Yellow Stone's Sacred Golden Eggs, not only for our village, but for all surrounding villages." Jasmine continued to stare into the deep well water, then said, "all right then, so be it. And it is so." She turned and walked away believing the answer would come to her.

Ivan thanked the well profusely and followed Jasmine down the path leading into the most beautiful garden he had ever seen. His breath was taken away by its beauty.

Jasmine was watching Ivan thank the well. She was impressed with his softness. She had seen him many times in war times, but this was the first to see him so humbled and gentle as he was standing in front of the well with such touching words of thanks.

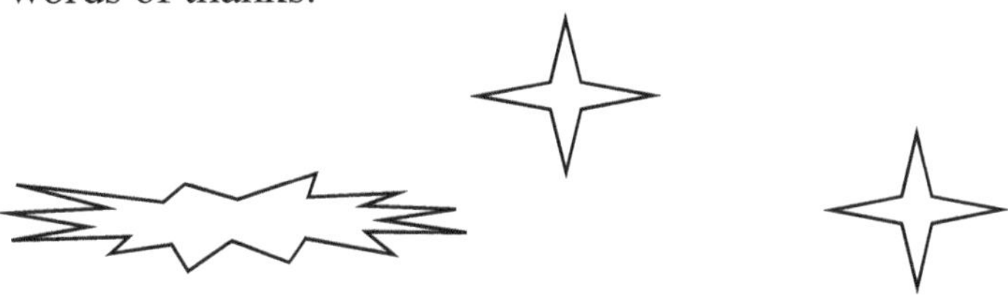

Ivan and Jasmine thanked Consa and left out through the gate.

They turned and waved and then quickly got on Breezy and Gallo and headed back to Valley of the Yellow Stones. The ride back was solemn. Neither spoke. They knew when the request was deeded; their lives would go back to normal. The eggs would be put in their rightful place and the village people would rejoice. They visioned it as they rode along the dusty path leading to the village.

As Jasmine and Ivan returned to the village, they both were solemn and Ramara could see right away that they had experienced something special and waited without asking what it was they had encountered at the Secret Garden. She had had a dream the night before that the eggs were found and returned and the village people had found their peace. She had awakened dampened from the sweat she encountered during the dream and walked to the water's edge and looked into the crisp, clear water and saw her place at Consa's Secret Garden. She knew it was time to leave the village and hand over her post to Jasmine.

Secret Garden

Chapter Twenty-One ☼

Ramara's Time to leave the Village

Jasmine looked into her grandmother's eyes, and knew it was time for her grandmother to leave the village. Her grandmother sent Jasmine a touching message of thought; *Granddaughter, the day has come to rest for a while from my recent journey and then we shall have a ceremony and you will take my place as Shaman.* Jasmine looked down at the ground and moaned silently to herself and sent back a thought to her grandmother; *Precious, oh precious, Grandmother, oh, how I will miss your nearness, but I am ready to replace your post as Shaman. I shall visit you often as you will me. I will be strong and think as a Shaman, as you have taught me. You will go to the secret garden of the ancient ones. You will be happy with your old friend, Consa, the gatekeeper, and Akish the guard lion. You will spend the rest of your days in a magical place where all ancient ones never age; they live on, forever.*

Ramara bent her head down, then lowered it between her knees and wept. She knew all those living in the secret garden would be safe and protected. The crisp, clear water told her it was time, showing her all animals that lived outside of the garden were the very ones who species had disappeared except for the ones remaining in the garden. They would never die. She was ready to go to the garden, ready to leave her post to her granddaughter, but she also knew, she'd miss seeing her on a daily basis.

The sun reaching up over the mountain caused a stir in Ramara, and she wanted to go to her granddaughter and tell her she was ready and would be packed within the hour. Ivan stood at the camp fire and looked out over the village with hope and love for it. He knew, he would never leave it. It was his home now. What that meant, he didn't know, but he did know, it was his home. He'd work to the bone to help bring all the village people together again; working and making Golden Stones for he knew thousands of years from now; thousands upon thousands, he would be one of the ancient ones. He would set a good example for the future children of this village. He would store history in the temple with more sacred eggs.

Ivan turned as Ramara touched his shoulder, and pulled her to him and whispered, "Your granddaughter will always be safe with me. I shall appoint myself as her guard. She will want for nothing. She will be happy. I will stand beside her, helping her to reach for the stars, and bring them down for letters in the history caves to demonstrate what a fine Shaman she was."

All packed and ready, they began their journey to Consa's Secret Garden. They had made it half way when a hummingbird approached them and right away Ramara said, "I know this hummingbird. His name is Simon. I'm sure he is here to give us a message. I fear something is wrong, or he wouldn't have greeted us so early."

Ramara watched him closely as he flew right up to her face, then darted back and forth until she asked, "Okay, Simon, I understand we are in danger. I see in my vision an insane bear up ahead. My sweet, little friend, thank you for letting us know to be aware."

They went on with their journey, and before long they heard growls and behind a tree out jumped a black bear with a white face and feet. He leaped on a soldier, knocking him to the ground and then killed him with one blow to the head. Jasmine lifted her sword and the bear instantly fell to the ground, paralyzed.

"This will be the last thing I'll do before going to the Garden. I've heard of this bear," Ramara said as she stood up and lifted her hand toward the bear and said, "*Remove this spirit from my sight - what is dark, shall be filled with light. Angels of protections, angels who hear - all those who don't belong here, all dark spirits; release thee as so it must be.*"

The bear began to move and then moaned as he turned into a male human, and quickly got up and said, "Oh, Shaman of the Valley of the Yellow Stones, thank you. You've removed the curse Sorcerer Valdmort put on me because I could not kill the bear that she turned me into."

"Very well, man, very well. Now go back to your village a free man without the heaviness of your curse," Ramara said and then sat back down.

The man bowed to Ramara, then turned and walked away. The morning was bright and the air crisp as they rode up on the mountain top toward Consa's Secret Garden when suddenly, two men rode fast toward them with singing in the air. Within several hundred feet away, Ivan could see Melody riding on Ruddey, and Hickey on her shoulder riding behind the two men.

They stopped within a few feet of Ivan and at that moment Jasmine, her grandmother, and Melody began singing the sweetest melodies they had ever heard. She lifted her arms to the sky, and let the notes ring out louder as the two men lifted the basket from their horses and handed it to Jasmine. She knew before she opened it, as did Ivan, that the rest of the eggs were in it, but she opened it and stared down into the basket while tears streamed down her face; there in a neat little row was the Sacred Golden Eggs. They sparkled and sent off a power that only Ramara had experienced, but now Jasmine felt it, lived it and became filled with the power. She lifted her arms up and sang with Melody as Ivan turned and looked at her, knowing she was the woman he would spend the rest of his day guarding; looking over her like a hawk would; glaring down to the ground from a high tree.

Ruddey, Hickey, and Melody took the eggs back to the Valley of the Yellow Stones, under Jasmine's orders while they continued on with their journey to Consa's Secret Garden.

"Look! I see the garden in the distance. Oh, it's so beautiful! I never get tired of its beauty. It's powerful!" shouted Jasmine as they journey on toward it. "I'm glad we decided to celebrate at Consa's instead of at the village. We shall celebrate the night away." Ramara said as they approached the gates.

The gates began opening, and there on the other side stood Consa and her lion, Akish, to greet them.

"Only those of pure heart may enter into my garden," Consa said as she held her walking stick. The large crystal on top sparkled with an eagle feather hanging from it. "Please enter."

As they entered a beautiful golden glow appeared and they walked through the gate.

Ramara, Ivan, and Jasmine went with Consa. Right away, Consa began telling them of the celebration she had planned gliding when the moon becomes full.

As they journeyed on deeper into the garden, Ramara saw dolphins standing on their tails greeting her while pods of whales came for a special greeting. The seals came closer and did a couple flips in the water in excitement, to see Ramara home at last.

High upon the mountain tops, snow laid in majestic white puffs of light. The very peaks of the mountain were shimmering while the sun was showering down on its beauty. The lush green hills everywhere in the garden, made one want to run and fall down to feel the greenness against the skin with its aliveness. Fruit trees filled - hanging with fruit that would bare its fruit all year long.

Omitheus the guardian, the centaur, who is half-human and half-horse of all the unicorns, ran toward them, excited that Ramara had finally made it home to share an eternity with them. Unicorns, Pegasus, and all the birds, ran to greet Ramara while the lush green grass swayed to the music of the flowers.

Consa strolled along with her arm in Ramara's while Jasmine glowed with happiness as she saw her grandmother glowing with joy, "I know you'll love your new home because it never gets cold here, Ramara, and the sun is warm, but never hot."

As Consa took Ramara, Jasmine, and Ivan through another part of the garden, they walked down paths lined with beautiful array of colorful flowers. Large rocks were covered with green moss and a variety of mushrooms set tightly against the rocks.

Jasmine walked in awe as she pointed to the trees. "Oh, look at the lushness of those trees. I don't believe I've ever seen such rich greenness before. Oh, Ivan, look at those picturesque flowers."

Birds of all kinds were gliding from branch to branch chirping as if in a conversation with one another.

Ivan smiled at Jasmine and bent down to smell the most tantalizing fragrance that sent him off in ecstasy. Ramara looked up at the large fluffy clouds hanging down like big white fluffy pillows in a dazzling blue sky.

Consa chuckled at their excitement as she stepped toward the center of the garden, which was very special. Ivan lifted his hand, and a little blue bird sit on it. He turned and looked at Consa and said, "Such a delicate little bird."

The bird looked up at Ivan and turned its little head from side to the other as if he understood what Ivan was saying, then gave out a few chirps and flew away. He landed in a nearby tree next to the path where Consa lead them over to. Over to the eastside set a small hill which was overlooking a turquoise scenic lake. In its bright, crisp, color, Ramara could easily see the different varieties of fish. Consa pointed out that all school of fish got along from the tiniest to largest.

Consa pointed to a long whispery, vine, hanging over a clay fence and said, “There is pure life in that vine and if you put it to your chest you will feel it pulsating with your own heart beat.” She stepped over and took a piece of the vine in her hand and said, “Smell the fresh air it sends out and feel what it is thinking. This is one of nature’s blessings to us and is what gives this garden life.”

Ivan bent down to smell the fragrance of the blossoms on the vine when a thousand butterflies soothingly flew down around them sending out energy like they had never experienced before. Ramara began giggling in her excitement and Jasmine turned and gave her a warm hug.

Ivan said, “Jasmine, look! These butterflies have a white light around them and they’re glowing.”

“Oh, Ivan, look at the rainbow colors gracefully floating out above them!”

Consa smiled at Ramara and said, “These butterflies are the spirit of the trees. They are gentle when they land upon a hand or shoulder. This is their way of saying, *welcome to the secret garden.*”

Ramara began smiling happily when she saw the different shapes and sizes of butterflies glowing with energy flying around and covering Jasmine’s body. Ivan was laughing out loud with happiness. Jasmine started to laugh too.

Ramara said, “they make us happy and fill our hearts with joy.”

“Be still and listen Ivan because they’re whispering a great wisdom to you.”

The four of them stood in the garden and became still as they listened. Consa reached out and touched the butterflies gently and said, “Yes, we hear you telling us to call upon you any time and you’ll be there for us.” She turned to Ramara and put an arm around her friend. “This is your home now, Ramara. It’s where life never dies and each time you see a butterfly remember they are there for you and send out good energy and a great presence of divine love that is never ending.

The butterflies began descending to the top of the tree.

Ivan and Jasmine stood speechless for a long while, and then began to walk back through the garden with Ramara and Consa. The four walked in silence feeling the powerful energy they had been given.

As they left the eastside of the garden, they entered into the northside, and that's when Ramara spoke with tears streaming down her face, "Oh, Consa, I feel balanced and whole already."

"Yes, my friend, we shall be together forever and what you see here will always look as it does now and the garden will thrive forever, including all those inside it."

After a few moments, Ramara walked over to Jasmine and placed a gentle kiss on her cheek and said, "Granddaughter, I will be happy here. Before you leave in the early morning hour, I wish to tell you that I have left a special wooden box at the village for you; knowing they'll be in good hands. You are now the new Shaman of the Valley of the Yellow Stones and a great healer of the village."

"Thank you, Grandmother. I shall visit you often," Jasmine said with tears in her eyes, but let's not speak of parting; let's talk about the celebration and all that we will experience when I come visiting you from time to time."

"You speak wisdom Granddaughter, but I have a few more things to say to you this day; you have much work to do in the world of the Vikons. The time will come, but not for many moons yet. I heard a voice in the winds that said you are wise and understand the power of the Universe, and that you are ready to step into my shoes. Always remember to give thanks for life. Never forget there will be times when your heart is heavy, but always remember to give thanks, even for those times; for it is pain endured – insight gained that counts.

Jasmine hugged her grandmother and said, “Thank you Grandmother.”

“You were a good pupil Granddaughter. You will teach the people to always give thanks to the universe into the innermost sanctuary in the spirit and in the truth.”

“Yes, I will, Grandmother. I remember all that you have taught me. I shall not let you down. I feel honored to be invited to step in your place and will try to do as you always did.”

“I have no doubt about that Jasmine. No doubts. But always remember, you will feel their hearts filled with heaviness in their pain and suffering, but you will heal them with your words of spiritual healing.” They embraced and soon after they heard Consa’s chimes begin to ring for the celebration to begin.

The tables were filled with all kinds of fruit and vegetables; rare that many had never seen before. Big purple looking plums as big as melons were in the center of the table and beside them were two platters of organic grapes of all different kinds and colors; red, green, yellow and blue. Vegetables that only those in the garden had seen; crisp clusters of beans of all kinds, carrots that were as sweet as honey and round shaped.

Ivan looked across the table at Jasmine, saw her excitement when she eyed the platter of berries of different flavors, as well as, different colors. They were plump, and juicy, and Ivan quickly began to fill a plate for her. She looked up at him when she saw what he was doing, and her taste buds became alive. He winked at her as he walked around the table and handed it to her.

“Eat till your stomach’s content this night of our celebration. If any of you wonder about the absence of meat; no animal dies in this garden. Drink to your heart’s content. Let’s welcome Ramara to our garden,” Consa’s sweet voice rung out for all around to hear.

By the time the celebration had gotten on its way, Melody, Ruddey and Hickey had arrived. Melody had brought her magical harp and began to sing while her magical instrument sent out tantalizing sounds which brought out hundreds of fairies. They traveled around like shining bright stars sparkling in the air. The power of the night had begun and all those in the garden were standing in awe of the magical voice and sounds Melody's Harp rang out to them all.

Melody began to sing with the full moon above her shining in its brightness. Everybody stood and listened while closing their eyes and hearing the melodies ring out so magically. Wine was flowing and people were in awe. "Come, friends. Come and dance. Enjoy the night," Melody called out to the people as she walked over to Ruddey and ask him for a dance as Jasmine and Ramara began their powerful singing. They lifted their arms to the heavens and bellowed out sounds that even surprised Jasmine and Ramara. Ruddey got so excited that he opened his mouth and out came fire, but it only went up and not a soul was touched. Hickey groaned and then simply smiled as she accepted a dance when the hummingbird flew over and began dancing around her and with her. She laughed and danced as they moved to the music.

Jasmine began to tell Ivan about all the animals in the garden and how they live forever. "Listen to the heart beat of all the animals. See that tiger lying over there on that plush vegetation? Look into his eyes and you'll know what he is thinking."

"Jasmine, this is a magical garden. I stand here in awe."

"We'll come back to visit Grandmother after she gets settled in and you'll learn oh so much more."

Consa held her arms out to the people and said, "Come, dance with me to the Elf ring circle of Life. Everybody get up and dance to the magic of the night."

Everyone got up and they created a circle while Melody was playing the harp and singing like an angel. They dance until the wee hours of the morning.

Chapter Twenty-Two ☼
Secret Garden and the Ending

Jasmine and Ivan departed feeling tired but content. They knew Ramara was happy with her new home at Consa's Secret Garden. Cosmos and Jazzel were snuggled up in their pouch exhausted from all the playing they did with the other creatures in the garden.

"It's hard leaving such a heavenly place. Grandmother will be happy and it's the right place for her," Jasmine said.

"The garden sure puts a magic spell on you," Ivan said as he gently pressed on Gallo's sides to move faster.

"Yes, it does. Grandmother told me after visiting Consa's garden it puts a magical spell on all who enter and once a human leaf, he leaves with a great spiritual responsibility to help others to become great light workers for humanity."

In the distance, Ivan heard screaming coming from a cave nearby. He rode up next to Jasmine and said, "Do you hear that scream?"

"Yes, where is it coming from?

Ivan pointed to the cave and said, "I think it's coming from the cave. Slow down and let me go check it out."

As he entered the dirt path leading to the cave, he saw a giant of a man, an ogre with a large club and his manic bull beside him.

He was terrifying the people who lived near the cave with his club. He would rise it up and strike several people with one flip of his hand. He had one eye that was cloudy, and some say he had the power of life and death. Ivan let out a long whistle and two shorts and Jasmine and Melody rode fast and hard to get to Ivan and when they got there, they climbed up the rocks to the cave entrance and saw that the Ogre had the village people corralled in a large pen while putting spells on them. Right away, Jasmine noticed the power was in his large club. One large swipe of his club was knocking the people down.

"Ivan if you'll distract the giant, I will go behind him," Jasmine whispered.

"Hey, you, big, Olaf, how about me; come and try your club on *Me*," hollered Ivan to the giant.

The giant turned, looked at Ivan, and started moving toward him while Jasmine got behind him with a large rope and tied it to the tree and motioned to the soldiers to help her cinch it up. "Magic rope, tie yourself around the giant's throat and take the magic from his hand." Jasmine sang.

The rope flew out in mid-air, wrapped itself around and around the giant, and he fell to the ground. Melody shot her arrow in the magic wooden club and he dropped it. The soldiers ran over and tied the giant up to the tree. Ivan out of breath from running said, "I need to catch my breath."

Jasmine started laughing and said, "That's the fastest I've ever seen you run. Oh, my sweet Ivan."

The soldiers released the villagers and Jasmine ordered a soldier to start a fire and when he did, she threw the club into the fire and it burnt to ashes.

A large woman ran over to Jasmine and said, "Thank you! That Ogre has terrorized our villagers for years. All of you are welcome to stay for our celebration tonight."

Jasmine released the giant ogre, and he promised to never hurt anyone again. Jasmine believed him because the spell had been released from him.

The village people ran ahead telling all the people of the event while shouting, "Celebration tonight! The giant's powers have been taken away. Come! Come people; prepare a big celebration for our guest!"

The women and men started preparations and found lodging for the guest. The music started and dancing began. The food was cooking on the live fire and the wine was being poured.

"We have so much to be thankful for this day. Our guest have saved us," The village leader cried out as he toasted to all who held a wooden cup of wine.

The next morning, Jasmine and the rest left for the Valley of the Yellow Stones feeling wonderfully happy and when they arrived, she looked around and knew she was now the shaman of her village and felt proud that her grandmother had prepared her well. Ivan put his arm around Jasmine and said, "The Valley of the Yellow Stones is going to be the best village around by the time we get through with the building and placing the Sacred Golden Stones in their rightful place."

Jasmine smiled and said, "Yes, it is because you are going to be here to make sure it is built well."

Ruddey flew up in the air and shouted, "I'm staying in the Valley of the Yellow Stones, are you Hickey?"

"Oh yes, Ruddey, I'm staying because you're my best friend and if you're staying, so am I."

Harpsong

With the dualism of the ocean, tender pastoral sigh and battle cry juxtaposed the music caressed forth by the bard's conjuring hand ignited a sonorous flame that sighed and roared in turns, like a subsiding tempest, silhouetted against the flames the soloist lent to the harp. The arachnid woven-chords wavered between introspective ... See Moresolitude and a loneliness as vast in its depths as the voids between the stars. Like two caravels passing in darkness spectral their gaze met with startling revelation. The dulcet Stradivarius strains mingled with then overpowered the mead halls writhing tendrils like charmed serpents. Resounding like crossed blades sparkingly, smiting each heart present tangibly and to the very essence of their being. A waking dream inspired a plaintive sigh akin to the expectant hush before the imminent maelstrom erupted. Each plucked, like individual stars drawn from the heights at his beckoning.

Written by Greg Patrick

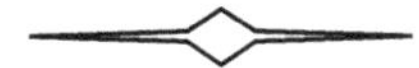

Valley of the Yellow Stones ll

See our next series of Valley of the Yellow Stones

www.ingramcontent.com/pod-product-compliance
Ingram Content Group UK Ltd.
Pitfield, Milton Keynes, MK11 3LW, UK
UKHW040601210726
13854UKWH00008B/1709

9 780359 572878